I0628179

INSIDE THE

WORLD

AS AL LEHMAN

MARVIN

COHEN

Sagging
Meniscus

© 1979, 2018 by Marvin Cohen
Book design © 2018 by Sagging Meniscus Press

Much thanks to Colin Myers for his assistance with preparing the manuscript.

All Rights Reserved.

Printed in the United States of America.
Set in Mrs Eaves XL with LaTeX.

ISBN: 978-1-944697-58-7 (paperback)
ISBN: 978-1-944697-59-4 (ebook)
Library of Congress Control Number: 2018930976

Sagging Meniscus Press
saggingmeniscus.com

INSIDE

THE

WORLD:

AS

AL

LEHMAN

AN INTRODUCTION

Who is Al Lehman? Keep reading. Maybe you'll find out.

I. THE EXCESSIVELY PRIVATE SOCIAL LIFE IN HIGH PUBLIC MASS DEMOCRACY, YET ON AN INDIVIDUAL BASIS, IN A LIFELONG CONTRADICTION OF SELF AND OTHERS.

Does Al Lehman have a story? He lives in a modern democracy. He struggles to be individual apart from the mass. Yet the mass is swallowing him up. Yet it spews him out, for it finds his individuality unassimilable.

Yet, it surrounds his individuality, and dictates terms to it, laying down conditions for regulating, compromising, containing, that little, unassimilable, indigestible lump of specificity by which Al Lehman has vaguely become characterized to the open public's broad indifference, despite his antics to convince them to notice, take heed, and become gripped in his private, unwitnessed drama.

He's lost. He can only be found by finding finders. This engages him, socially, in all his involvements. In his ritual of "Look! Look! I'm me!"

A few look. They comprise his world. They listen. They take him in. He counts, to them. They're his existence's founders, underwriters, advocates, endorsers. They constitute the grounds for his identity. They establish him. But they demand that *he* look, that *he* listen. They assert, enforce, themselves. They tangle up Al Lehman. They're his threads of social fabric. He daren't go threadbare. He needs them; they respond if they need him. He's a peopled person, in his own right.

And *they*'re peopled, partly by him. He's only a part of anyone else's entire social life. But anyone else is only a part of his. Part meets part: each is party, then, to a partnership.

That's only partly true. What *isn't* true, though, isn't neces-sarily false; it simply doesn't apply.

Truth is fitness, aptness: what applies. Al Lehman himself is a body of truth. It's magnetized, and magnetizes. It attracts what belongs to it; and *is* attracted, to what *it* applies to.

Woven in a social network. People get on and off his life, like passengers, at odd stations, on a moving train. It roars or slows down. He's a peopled vehicle. He peoples *others'* trains. The tracks cross. The schedules conflict. Crashes. Derailments. Those engines of driven energy. On courses of cooperative col-lision.

II. AL LEHMAN, THE FATHERED FUTURE FATHER

Al Lehman pondered his own origins. They had conspired, his origins, through tumultuous accident, in a casual random through an interwoven series of events, to produce his own self, his mortal body.

He had come from the past. And was now contributing to the formation of another person's past. Whose? His unborn son's.

His son Gregory. From his wife Marge, whom he hadn't met yet.

It lay ahead.

Stretched behind lay his network of origins. Continuity spanned itself through him, its latest link, extending vital origins through time's personal renewal.

III. AL LEHMAN'S SELF: AS AN ADJECTIVE TO CONSCIOUSNESS, OR AS A NOUN TO HIS OWN SOLID OBJECTIVITY? AS REFLECTION, OR AS EXISTENCE? AS AN IDEA FLUX, OR AS AN IDENTICAL IDENTITY TO HIS OWN PURE SELF?

Thinking about thinking was so self-reflective, that Al Lehman could barely do as he was, or be as he did, since his feelings were thinking about the thinking that reflected the non-definition by which his identity had lost itself.

After due deliberation, he snapped back to being and doing, having shed the veils of consciousness that had so elaborated the simple constancy of his own consistency.

Back he was, to being Al Lehman, acting accordingly. He had regained his self as his own private noun. It had served as an adjective to consciousness, during which time he had personally found himself to be lost.

Back to being Al Lehman, who survived being self-consciously reflected.

Back to the self as a self.

But self-consciousness clung to him. He wasn't *only* Al Lehman. He was a portrait of Al Lehman in the process of self-reflecting thought. No more was he merely a solid mass, a hunk of pure Al Lehman.

Thinking annihilated him. To all the what in ever his mental matter.

IV. THE AL LEHMAN THAT NO MIRROR CAN DISPLAY

Al Lehman looked for himself in the mirror; but all he saw was an image.

"That's not me," he pointed out.

"But it's how you seem," answered the mirror-reflection.

"Only how I seem to *me*. But just what is that 'me,' which that reflection seems before? Mirrors are no help, on that score. They only blind the issue, by a blaze of appearance. Superficiality is worse than nothing, for it misleads."

Thus complained Al Lehman: the Al Lehman who wasn't there, in his own mirror, despite some outward semblance of himself neatly splattered on the bright-eyed glass.

V. THE ACTIVE WORLD IN ITS SLEEPING MIRROR

What happened to the world while Al Lehman was asleep? It kept orbiting. It turned slowly on its annual course of revolution, in cycle to seasonal phase. People went about doing or non-doing what they were all about anyway, in stages of sleep or wake. Meanwhile, while Al Lehman slept through all this, the turning world on which Al Lehman slept kept up its slow revolution.

It seeped through to Al Lehman's sleeping consciousness— which turned and revolved to the same rhythm. He mirrored in miniature the very outside orb in faithful semblance and true fiery duplicate.

His was a mental earth—continuous with the physical one that sprawled outside.

Dream-films played on his mental earth's all-around screen. His little life was rounded with a sleep. The vast earth kept seeping through. He turned, it gyrated him. He was host to universal consciousness. Or kept local outpost to its far-flung network. It kept channeling in through his station. The reception was clear, clean, and humming. It radiated and buzzed through all his fibers. He was one, with all.

VI. WHAT IS AL LEHMAN'S PLACE IN SPACE, WHILE HE'S THERE? DOES HE *KNOW* HIS PLACE, WHILE OCCUPYING IT? AND WHAT ABOUT EVERYWHERE ELSE, AT THAT TIME? TO WHAT USES ARE THEY PUT?

"Other people begin where my flesh ends. If I put on weight and get a little fatter, then other people have to begin a little further away from me. But I'm not trying to elbow them out of existence. There's space enough for all of us. The margin between them and me, or 'border line' to use a geographical metaphor, is the fleshy contours of myself, the edge of my very skin, though usually in a clothed state. My corporeal body, of course, is matter. No-one else can take up the space *it* takes up—except before or later, such as in a grocery store or in a movie queue or on the toilet or in the bathtub or on the subway or just standing on a street corner. They're welcome to the space I vacated—anyone is who qualifies—or to the space I *will* occupy, provided they get out of the way once I come barging in."

The outside world begins where Al Lehman ends. Europe and America begin where the Atlantic Ocean ends. The above paragraph was written by Al Lehman, about the priorities of space where he's concerned. The same applies to his grave-plot. No-one else's set of bones may occupy the space carved out for Al Lehman's. Earlier on, no-one else occupied his mother's womb except embryonic Al, at the time she was carrying him. He moves in privileged space, unique in his rights. Others, then, keep out of his way. They have to, if they don't want to "get under his skin."

But a demon occupies him. And a love resides in his heart. When he goes about, he contains them. He bears them. They can't be knocked out from their places, inside him, save by their successors that will replace them.

Nor can Al Lehman be knocked out of *his* place, while the earth contains his body, till either before or after his going or coming in full self.

The earth itself occupies vast space, surrounded by distance. But what the earth may *bear*. . .

VII. THE SECONDARY AND DERIVATIVE FAME IN KNOWING FAMOUS PEOPLE—THE UNTALENTED MAN'S ROAD TO TRUE CELEBRITY STATUS.

Al Lehman's dream was, that if he couldn't become famous by himself, at least he'd be well recognized and warmly greeted (in public, before people's amazed eyes) by those who are truly famous, whose fame would then rub off on him, giving him a derived or secondary fame, a reflected glory somewhat different from the moon's, but somewhat similar too, since the moon's silver pallor is by roundabout way of that central star of the firmament, the sun.

"If only people could envy me by seeing famous people greet me and shake my hand with a personal glint of warmth and an intimate wink of sparkle that openly and publicly credits me with being the familiar and intimate on unique terms of exclusive equality with those famous ones, whose renown is universally accredited but whose inner personalities include me by natural affinity in their private circles of rare brotherhood."

Thus wished Al Lehman, starting to cultivate acquaintanceships leading to friendships with those either already famous or with those likely to be—in fact, with both of those thoses, as he built his present and his future together.

This was after Al Lehman seriously or unseriously tried hard or softly to become famous in his own right, in literature, art, television, and journalism, in advertising, public relations, commerce, athletics, religion, and politics; but he failed in all of those ambitious fields, failed almost systematically, even indiscriminately, wielding his special talent for failure which occasionally amounted practically to genius, in the art of judicious failing at ambitions or careers for which, alas, he lacked requisite aptitude, however hard he tried, with diligence, perseverance, and ultimately unrewarding struggle. True failure is never without real effort and attempt. By that definition, Al Lehman definitely complied with those standards.

To shine by compensation, he developed his gift for being seen in the company of famous people and basking in the public radiance of their limelight, sharing and partaking of their glory, arousing curiosity, resentment, envy, toward himself by the mobs of idolizing strangers.

Eventually, he himself was being interviewed, as a species of conspicuous sub-celebrity, making a ubiquitous reputation at special events which were so frequent.

He was always successfully hovering around the famous, and going off with them to private parties following public events; to their own very homes after small but select parties; in their actual company, accompanied by them. He was interviewed on television, radio, in newspapers and periodicals, and was asked to disclose the secrets of the mighty which had been confided in him; but he never betrayed these secrets, he always kept those confidences, and thus, an aura of mystery, stubborn intriguing honesty, tantalizingly clung to him.

His was a species of sub-celebrity that was gradually donning hero status. How great it was, in those days, to be Al Lehman, in such select company!

He was in his borrowed glory, galore. He was on the outer fringes of magnificent radiances, yet, somehow, "in the know," with his ears to the lips and hearts of the mighty.

As Horatio was to Hamlet, so was Al Lehman to those stars of sports, show business, politics, television, books, opera, ballet, theater, glamor, high society, movies, art, culture, entertainment, and just about anything that compelled public admiration and clamor. He became the right-hand man of the well celebrated.

Then, one by one, an epidemic or plague grew into fashion, of dropping Al Lehman. All the famous people who knew him got into that act. The fashionable thing to do, the chic and trendy thing to do, was to drop Al Lehman; and that's what all his famous "friends" did. They all got in on that act. Dropping him was popular—a status symbol. You just weren't a star, unless you dropped Al Lehman. The famous ones who didn't already know him quickly took him up and in a whirlwind befriended him, in order to be able, then, to drop him.

His ego was bruised—badly. Oh, what a thing to do! Poor Al Lehman. How his star had fallen—all over the place. He was held up—or down—to public contempt.

He was scorned, and ignored—the ultimate insult. This cured him of his obsession for fame. It reduced him, to a non-snob. Fame came to spurn him; his revenge, is to hold fame in contempt. That's the current occupation of his talent. He's very successful, at it—adept just to the point of genius, in being immune to the fame germ.

No-one who's anyone knows him, any more. He snubs those who snub him. A perfect arrangement, on all sides. Fame is doing very well without him, thank you; and he without it. He's wild about *simple* things, instead, and has become passionately private. His privacy requites his passion. They're a perfect pair, he and his privacy. They keep well out of the limelight, avoid its glare altogether, in the modesty of their romance.

VIII. TO BE A WRITER? TO BE A FAMOUS AUTHOR? TO LABOR AT THE BOOK. SUBMIT IT. SUBMISSIVELY. TO GOALS OF LOVE AND GLORY.

Being a "writer" kept occurring to Al Lehman as an ever-recurring possibility. As a successful author, there would be fame, money, and women in store, those heartwarming rewards for talent and hard work.

A best-selling novel would do the trick. Of course, there yet remained the business of writing it.

How would he set about it? It's not a thing to be lightly done.

Inspiration would have to be found, and genius closely approximated.

Then again, the question of "content" took on paramount proportions. His theme should have a "bite" in it, to grab the reader by the interest.

A subject of universal appeal would furnish the "matter." As for "manner," style would take care of that. Form would wrap together those two ingredients, in a shapely bundle.

He rummaged through his own personal history (of which there had been so much!), hoping to come across some autobiographical material from which to glean some salient angle, a key event to touch off a verbal torrent from his slashed-open sky bulging with endless imagination.

Of course, there should be plenty of sex in the book. Otherwise, how compete in a commercial market for popular readership?

Sex should rear its controversial head from—at least—every other page.

Honest, raw, gusty, lusty—straight from the heart.

No coy hypocrisy here. But open, unabashed. From his pure and aching gut.

Defying censorship—even if censorship still existed. But the book market had rid itself of that.

Freedom was a big boost for business. Al Lehman would ride it high, to fame, popularity, success—and love for himself by women of youth and glamor, who would offer him the closest intimacy that their bodies could afford—sex, liberally flavored with love's heady aroma.

He fell into a swoon of intoxication, in reverie over these contemplations. Such giddy longings were now dizzied over by hope's actual promise.

What title would the book bear?

Leave that till later. First, what's the book to be *about*?

He'd begin Chapter One. May God guide his hand. His head was a pure study in emptiness.

A fertile nothingness, teeming to pregnant abundance.

A *book* was in him. It would come out not wholesale, but word by following words, one slow bit at a time.

Had he anything to say?

Either nothing, or too much.

More than nothing, but less than too much, became his particular aim. As yet a bit broad, or vague.

But he was drawing closer.

Once close enough, he'd pounce and clutch. To grab and make. To make, and have. A finished manuscript. To agent, to publisher, to public, to social and literary history, posterity, immortality, fame.

And women's love. In the rusty prime of his own lifetime.

Love and art. Life and work. Glory, magnificence, beauty.

Put those ideals aside. Now write a modest first draft of words. Start, humbly, on his anonymous paper.

Apply the pen. String words together. Commit a few phrases.

Cross out, or correct, at times. Fill pages. Become absorbed. Lose yourself.

Years later, wake up to a new dream. A modest first novel. Gently dismissed by the critics. But showing high promise. Enough to try again. Risk failure, or a lukewarm brush with success. Find your own wife to marry: one who'd marry *you*— not your book.

Struggle. Work hard. Give. The goals grow dimmer. Words load the pages. Characters, setting, details, dialogue, plot, built up.

Years at the words. The story is padded with sex.

But the manuscript isn't sold.

The publishers all turn it down.

Al Lehman is married, with a child.

Office job. Divorce. Problems. Complications. An unpublished writer. An unwanted script. Collapsed love.

Son goes with mother. Al Lehman is alone. In a new bachelor flat. With the old office job.

Modest circumstances. No fame.

He dates women, he goes out.

No more writing. He's failed.

No more attempt.

The dusty manuscript. In the bureau drawer. Fading, with time.

IX. A POET BEMOANS HIS UNPUBLISHED STATE. HIS POETRY CHOKES HIM, BECAUSE NO BOOK BEARS IT. POOR POET. HIS PAST INSPIRED PRIVACY CRAVES EXPOSURE, IN PRINT'S POPULAR DAYLIGHT.

"I must wait for the world to catch up," moaned a sadly neglected poet who was woefully unpublished.

Al Lehman didn't know whether to sympathize or not: he would if the poet was *undeservedly* neglected. "If you're a good poet, why doesn't the world recognize you?"

"Because I haven't been published."

"Is that the fault of your poetry, or of the publishers?"

"The publishers, who don't recognize a good thing when they see one. Some do, in my case, but they consider my manuscript too utterly rare to inflict upon the gross, beastly public. Publishers, then, arbitrate public demand, anticipate popular response, to a prospective work. They intermediate, between me the poet, and the reading populace out there. Their intermediation, in my case, is obstructively negative, and destroys my very chances of being openly introduced in print and circulated to the light of day for the right readers to discover."

"But you've been in magazines, at least."

"Only those of frail circulations. I need a massive readership. An entire book of my work, to reach the general bookstore market. Only then, could my work prove itself."

"Genius often does go unnoticed, till almost or all of its owner's lifetime has run itself, unobserved, out."

"I'd like earlier attention than all that, and lots of it."

"Don't a select few appreciate you?"

"Yes, but I want the circle to widen, with a book that pursues anonymous strangers through many copies."

"Then keep submitting to publishers, get printed in more magazines, get more widely known through readings, and construct more manuscripts for further submissions."

"That's a practical program, but I already follow it."

"Then my advice is redundant."

"Goodbye, Al Lehman—do *you* like my poetry?"

"I haven't read it. I don't want to read it in magazines or manuscript or hear it at readings. I'm waiting for a whole *book* to be published, officially, commercially, of it."

"So am I, Al Lehman. You a reader, and me the maker. We need that one breakthrough: an authentic bound book's public print of my past inspired privacy: a deep plunge into dear exposure's outer daylight, an unimpeded outpouring into the impurity of other minds."

"Like mine."

"*Typically* like yours, Al Lehman: you're any poet's final challenge."

X. THE MYSTERY OF EXISTENCE. WHAT DOES AL LEHMAN DO ABOUT IT? OR *DOES* HE, EVEN?

The mystery of existence has always, of course, fascinated Al Lehman.

But what could he *do* about it?

Not much, really. It was just *there*. That was his only adjustment, deal, arrangement, relationship, attitude, stance, posture, approach, he could take, in regard to it.

He let it be. He actually let the mystery of existence go on being! How excessively kind of him, so benign, so fatherly!

The mystery of existence thanks him. From the very bottom of its "heart," or middle of its "soul," or center of its "essence," or "spirit"'s brimming core, the mystery of existence extends cordial thanks to Al Lehman for permitting it —nay, encouraging it—to be!: to be, in all its mighty majesty, in all its careless magnificence, its boundless universality on all sides.

Al Lehman is the proprietor, entrepreneur, or manager, or lion-tamer, or circus master, of the mystery of existence.

The mystery of existence doesn't know this—or pretends not to. This grants Al Lehman immense liberty, to play his role.

It's a private, inward drama. Such subjectivity, which the mystery of existence is debarred from, or privy to.

It goes on. *Al Lehman* goes on. One, assuming its broad course; the other, his own pretensions, preoccupations, dreams, assumptions.

When *he* stops, the other will *remain* the mystery of existence. There's no lack of people for the mystery of existence to "play itself" upon. No lack, whatever.

XI. WHEN DOING DOESN'T AVAIL, WILL PRAYING DO?

Al Lehman went to church when he was in trouble. He prayed when something was wrong. He became superstitious when a problem bothered him that he couldn't solve. But when things were all right, he didn't need church, prayers became unnecessary, and acts of superstition were suddenly seen to be irrational.

What was controllable through his own agency, he exerted control upon; what he could alter, modify, improve, in the conditions of his life, his situational circumstantiality: he did what he could to bring about what was more desirable, reduce what was dissatisfying, tame and harness his social environment in line with his own goals and prospects.

He acted; was acted upon; and knitted his way through a semi-yielding world, whose objects would so contrarily object, whose obstacles would just as suddenly relent; events would turn accidental; happenings emerge from flux and confusion; contingency held arbitrary sway; nor could mercy be obtained from a cold and ruthless objectivity, except by lucky turn, the tricky prank of "fate" reversing chills and ills to warm health's respite, life surging upward.

To have influence over people; to cooperate; to be kind; to request; to respond.

People gave in; compromised; had their way; bartered; bargained; granted or demanded concessions. Al Lehman was in amongst them, giving, taking, acting, being acted on. Things were worked out; abandoned; started up again; left alone; considered; dealt with; treated, with this or that method.

What was impossible, beyond action being taken on, outside control, had to be left up to chance. If anxiety persisted, and worry kept irritating: superstition, religion, prayer, God, conciliatory gestures with magic repetition that placated for intervention, became resorted to, in the throes of helpless fear of a social world gone out of control with alarm and peril, the demonic anarchy of lawless chance. Help is pleaded for; protection clamored for; so frail can action be, at times: ineffectual means; bootless resources; at the end of wits' extremity.

To cause; or, if action fails, then, to appeal to the good chance of change to brighten the circumstance and thaw out a rigid situation in desire's favor, flowing out toward a sea of advantage, on opportunity's thrilling tide. On waves of prosperity. Released swelling full on the bounty of good fortune. Sweeping dark adversity aside. Hope and optimism, glowing down.

XII. TO SUNDAY THE WHOLE WEEK

Almost anything on a Sunday is a contradiction to itself, except a church.

A church is in full force, on Sunday. Sunday not only becomes it, but is the condition for its fulfillment.

But a *store* is not itself on a Sunday: it's closed.

A business office, on a Sunday, is totally nullified. It just isn't what it is. It's Sundazed.

A school, on a Sunday, simply *isn't*. The answer to the question "When is a school not a school?" can be easily researched by the researcher's trying to enter a school by ringing the bell or knocking on the door when—and get the time right—it's Sunday.

A church booms on Sunday, it really comes into its own. Al Lehman was able to confirm this. He attended church last Sunday, and got a complete service out of it. Religion and Sunday have become permanently associated in the mind of anyone who's a member of our culture. Whoever are the exceptions, Al Lehman isn't one of them.

In private fantasy of power and might, he secretly sees himself as God, only no-one knows it. It's the most supreme delusion of grandeur that mortal can conceive, the omnipotence of a deity.

It's his pet and fond illusion, which he has the discipline to refrain from indulging except only on a Sunday, which makes him a dilettante dabbler as a divinity, not wholly such, but holiday-holy, not committed, not dedicated, but setting aside the appropriate day and donning his assumed role, like an actor who knows he's really not what he's acting but who, while cast in that role, believes it on the stage, when the theater is in session. Then, the character that he fits is truly himself.

Al Lehman is only a Sunday God. However, everyone else is not even that.

Does he nourish an ambition to go into it full-time? No, his aspirations keep modestly down-to-earth, where he knows his humble station, on all but Sunday.

He's planning, however, to make *every* day a Sunday, without exception. This would increase his empire, and expand his power, to the utmost dominion.

But commerce, industry, and schools—when could they be active, in a world of nothing but Sunday? This problem needs some ironing out. It's secular and societal, in scope, and even, somehow, outside religion's jurisdiction.

Al Lehman can't solve it yet. But he'll grapple with it on Sunday.

He's trying to summon his faith, for such a task. To reconcile the worldly secular acts of mankind with the holy, if all take place on the same holy day, without diminishing its holiness. Society, economics, and such other workaday customs, those essential occupations that keep things going, must be kept going. How, though, by all that's holy?

Today it's Sunday. But the problem is unsolved. Al Lehman fails. He succumbs to doubt. Self-doubt, an almighty failing, in his sovereign case.

XIII. AL LEHMAN, WHO PLOTS TO KILL THE GOD HE'S STILL PRAYING TO.

"Whatever's there, knock it down," thought Al Lehman. "For example, Christianity's there, it's become overestablished, it's a bulky bulwark, a petrified citadel, a doomed old dowager, an ossified dummy's fossil, an eroded old ramparts.

"It's outused its own shape. It enjoys a phony survival. It's confusing its lingered sunset for its historically valid sunrise, and cripples the horizon with an artificially kept-alive heap of crumbling mold.

"I'll kick it down, and Judaism too. Christians and Jews are meaningless labels that encumber more than they identify.

"Down with God, he's been around too long. He's a legend worn inside out by a hollow shell.

"Down with mankind, too. It leans against us people, and weighs us down.

"What should remain up, after such wholescale razing and leveling by the fine destructive frenzy of all this sweeping wrath?

"People, to start anew. On the refuse mound of tradition, they'd scavenge for useful remnants.

"Disburdened of religious raiment. Free, to propel a new race of future souls on this burial-covered earth."

Having discharged himself of these principles, Al Lehman knelt down with a free heart. He worshiped the god he was soon to destroy, like fattening a calf into a holy cow full of true meat, soon to be foully slaughtered, and brought cooked to the high feast.

XIV. COLLECTING PHONE NUMBERS OF WOMEN MET AT A PARTY, WITH SEXUAL GOALS IN MIND IN EACH CASE. THEN PHONING THEM, WITH RESULTS TABULATED FOR YEARS THEREAFTER.

The women whom Al Lehman saw at the party appealed to him, for various reasons, all of them sexual. He would collect the phone numbers of those he felt so strongly about; so that the party would be the mushrooming nucleus to a scattering of assorted love affairs owing source and origin to this great meeting ground.

Years went by. He finally exhausted those phone numbers and himself. Some of the women had in the first place refused to give him their phone numbers. Others had given him their phone numbers but had turned down his request for a date when he phoned, or put him off and made him phone again, but always with the result that he never ever saw them again.

Other women, recruited from that party via phone numbers, had responded and made appointments but saw him only once or a few times and then never again.

A few of the women from that party saw him more often, until they too stopped seeing him, eventually.

A few saw him over long stretches of time, until gradually the meetings stopped with them too.

None were left, from the original batch of phone numbers.

There had been nothing sexual with any of them, as it all turned out.

Original motivation; but consequences of a quite different order.

Such intriguing possibilities, at that party. All declined, in time's full stop.

XV. THE REWARDS FOR HIGH RISKS, THE DULL ASSURANCE FOR LOW RISKS

Al Lehman risked liking a girl, just liking her; so that, when her rebuff came, it seemed gentle, easy to take.

Liking wasn't much of a risk. Loving is a great risk. So he loved a girl, and risked *really* getting hurt. He did get hurt. To the extent of his love and how long its hope was allowed to develop how high.

How much hope and desire should he invest in what? He was an emotional speculator. Losses and gains developed, on the sites of his buildings.

The unexpected defies the experience of wisdom. So he goes on, trusting to the unknown, or distrusting when pessimistic. Piled high with surprises, his life hasn't allowed any formulas to survive unmodified. With educated plunges, he blunders on.

XVI.

(Title sums up, so it's best placed after what it sums up, which has to go first:)

Al Lehman was trying to improve his appearance, to make a better impression on Clara, to whom he took a shining fancy, to which she responded with total indifference. "Nothing you do would make the slightest difference to me," said she, discouragingly. "Alter yourself, change yourself, it'll do you no good, you'll go through all that trouble for nothing, for its own sake, for it won't affect me the slightest, you simply don't appeal to me, you're just not my type, I can't help it, I just wasn't made to take to you, you can dance on your head all day long and it won't get a rise out of me. Sorry to have to put it so bluntly. I'm kind enough to hate to see you go through all your vain efforts, for my sake. I'm sorry to see you waste yourself. Better try somewhere else. Some other girl may respond."

"Some *other* girl! I only crave *you!*"

"Don't be so mulish. Give up, I'm a lost cause for you. Better results could be obtained elsewhere."

"Can *you* become someone else, Clara? Then I'd woo the someone else that you'd become. It wouldn't be *you* any more, but at least it would be *derived* from you. That way, I could maintain my passion, seeing that you're the source for the someone else. Isn't that a grand solution?"

"Theoretically, it may be. But I'll remain me. I *can't* become another girl."

"You *can't*, or you *don't want* to?"

"Both. So give me up. Accept total rejection, from me, unqualified, unconditional. Weep a little, then get over me."

"Goodbye, Clara. I see, now, that this must be the end."

"How very intelligent of you, Al. Or perceptive. Or both."

"Don't make fun of me, please."

"A little fun, at your expense? It's really quite harmless. You cut a ridiculous figure. You've wooed me in vain. Only now, your failure has dawned upon you—at my urging. You're a silly ass."

"It's unkind of you, to humiliate me."

"I can't spare your pride and vanity. They took the risk, in my cause, and have become compromised. Go repair your pride and vanity with a girl who'll love you—one, furthermore, whom *you*'ll love. How much better that will be, in all respects, for all concerned, than your dismal failure with *me!*"

"Your point, Clara, is well made. I abandon all hope, for you. Farewell, lost love."

"Goodbye, you fool."

(The summing-up title:)

CLARA CONVINCES AL LEHMAN, A BIT ROUGHLY, THAT THE PASSION HE'S CONCEIVED FOR HER WOULD DO HIM NO GOOD, SINCE SHE CARES NOT A WHIT FOR HIM, AND NOTHING HE DOES CAN MAKE THE SLIGHTEST DIFFERENCE IN ALTERING HER CONFIRMED, ABSOLUTE, TOTAL, AND COMPLETE INDIFFERENCE TO HIM. SO, SINCE HE CAN'T INFLUENCE HER, SHE INFLUENCES HIM. HIS PRIDE REELS, UNDER THE BLOW. TIME, THOUGH, WILL SEE HIM THROUGH, TO HIS EVENTUAL RECOVERY. AH, CLARA: GOODBYE.

XVII. ON THE PHONE WITH A LOVED ONE

"You mean you still haven't received my letter, yet?" said Doris, over the telephone.

"No. When did you send it?" asked Al Lehman, anxiously—also on the phone. Their communication, on that occasion, was one hundred percent by phone. Other than the letter that Doris said she sent but which Al Lehman, to his alarm, hadn't received yet, that was their sole means of communication, for months.

This limitation was imposed by Doris. Although she wouldn't say why, she was mad at Al Lehman, and simply refused to see him. He was permitted, twice a week, to speak with her by phone.

What had he done? She wouldn't tell him. For some unknown reason, he was being punished.

He was being treated unfairly. Well, why wasn't he rebelling? He loved Doris, which gave her the upper hand and allowed her to set arbitrary rules at her whim's tyranny. He had to submit, in the hope, one day, that she'd yield herself over, and be sweetly his by his own unlimited terms.

"I sent you the letter two weeks ago."

"It must have gotten lost in the mail. If I haven't gotten it by now, then I'll probably never get it. What was in it? What had you written?"

There was that anxious screech in Al Lehman's voice, a beseeching yelp or whine, like a pathetic dog petitioning its dog-hating keeper for a bone bald of the barest meat.

"I'm not telling you what I wrote. If you ever get that letter, you'll find out. If not—you'll never know."

"That's cruel, Doris; and unfair. If you wrote and mailed the letter properly, then you *wanted* me to know what you were saying, right? Then to deprive me now is senseless. From your own will, you wrote me certain things. It's an accident of the post office that I don't know what you wrote. If you *intended* me to know what you wrote, then please, use this phone that we're on, and tell me over it."

"No."

"Why?"

"You're too anxious. You're too eager. So instead of intending you to know, I intend you *not* to know. I'm glad of the post office accident. I won't relieve your anxiety or eagerness. I like to see you squirm."

"But you're not *seeing* me squirm. If you wish to—let's arrange to meet, in person. The phone is blind, and our voices have no bodies. If only I could see your face and expression!"

"If you could, you'd see unkindness on it, toward yourself. But even of *that* dubious pleasure, I deprive you. I refuse to meet you. I refuse to divulge what was in the letter. I take pleasure, in general, of being on a refusing policy with you. Next, I forbid you to phone me for another three weeks. Should you disobey, I'll cut off *all* communication, forever. My message must be plain, so I'll hang up."

"No! Why are you torturing me? What did I do to you, to deserve this?"

"You committed the great indiscretion of loving me. That places you, like a fool, under the sway of my rather negligent mercy, I'm afraid. I derive quite a perverse joy, in tormenting you so. For you alone, I'm so empowered. No-one else is so unwise, as to love me. Go on loving me. I love it—not you, but being loved. I love my authority. I love to rule. You don't *dare* get out of hand; for then I'll further withdraw my permission for your tiny liberty to contact me. I'm blind with this power over your major fears, your wildest hopes. Sing and dance for me, Al Lehman. You jump and slide, to my strings. I play you, up and down."

Doris's gloating tones were on a telephone key of triumph. Al Lehman had one fear, now: that she'd hang up. Then he was disallowed to phone her for three weeks again. He hoped to stall her hanging up. Dare he mention the letter again? He tremored, in her power. Had he no pride to reverse such weakness? He couldn't bear losing her. Some day, she'd yield him all her love. Then would revenge be possible. Till then, he bowed in captivity. He'd wait her out. They'd switch positions, *she*'d love *him*. He'd punish her, brutally.

XVIII. LOVE, AND "MAKING" LOVE: TWO THINGS, SOMETIMES RELATED, SOMETIMES NOT, IN VARIED HUMAN UNDERTAKINGS.

Janet loved Al Lehman, giving him the opportunity to *make* love to her, which he was far from slow to do.

Gradually, though, he loved her too. The more he began loving her, the less and less became her love for him, until the point was reached where he felt all the love and she felt none. All that while, they had been "making" love.

At the point when Janet felt no love for him, and he all for her, she decided to "pull out" from their union. Such pain he felt! All the pain was his; the relief was hers.

Finally, he "got over" her. He's finally joined her, in their lasting indifference, which is the final state of affairs between them.

Janet is "making" love with a new man, now: a man whom she doesn't love, and who doesn't love her.

Al Lehman is "making" love with a new woman, whom he doesn't love. She's Judy. She's growing to love him. Will her love for him influence the growth of some love for her, in him? Time will tell. They "make" love, while waiting.

XIX. TO BELONG, NOT TO BE ALONE, TO JOIN, TO BE IN WITH, TOGETHER WITH, A PART OF, A PARTY TO, AT THE PARTY, AMONG THE OTHER GUESTS, ONE WITH ALL; FOR ALL THAT ALL IS NEEDED TO CONSOLE THE SPLIT-OFF NARROW TERROR OF BEING ONLY ONE, IN OVERWHELMING ISOLATION FROM TOO MUCH.

People congregating: that's an excitement for Al Lehman. He's just divorced, and in addition has broken up with an interim girlfriend. He's as lonely as a foreigner who can't speak or understand the language of the country he's suddenly and solitarily been exiled to without a single connection there, a stranger's unrelieved gloom among crowds of natives who glow with belonging to each other, from whom that stranger is kept endlessly alien, an outsider forbidden to partake, always ever only apart.

Wherever people congregate, Al Lehman, if he can, shows up: even when uninvited. Often, invitations are unnecessary. He's becoming ubiquitous. Depend on it, he's there, if there's a social event to which advance notice drew his attention.

A wake, a christening, a wedding, a memorial service, and there he is, adding his "one" to the attendance.

A lecture, a poetry reading, a concert, and the audience may be seen to include him. Even when he's not interested in the subject lectured on, the poetry being read, the music heard, or whatever demonstration or performance there is as pretext to join a public or even private gathering. He's there, as *though* he's interested—which he's not, in most cases. He has a social disease: he mustn't be alone. Even death seems preferable to a horrible evening of solitude.

Known friends and acquaintances don't suffice if they're already known. He requires larger groups, and strangers, the unknown, a social adventure. He takes his chances. He risks morbid non-belonging, by being drawn, obsessively, compulsively, to any and all occasions for a gathering that avail his opportunity to attend when meeting his notice, however briefly in advance he finds out about these events.

"There he is again," people whisper. "Who is he? He seems out of place, here. What's he doing here? Why is he here? Is he a spy? A reporter? A crazed solitary, desperate for remote companionship, crowding his lonely isolation with people as stage props, background configurations incidental but necessary to his autistic, withdrawn, hermetic, sealed-off, doomed, tragic apartness, his exile from his spiritual kind?"

He courts rejection, everywhere, by his urgent eager note of desperation, that panting, craven urgency obvious to all calmer people. He's a maniac, a self-destructive, self-imposed leper. A social leper, because of, despite of, his blatant attempts not to be.

He bungles; he blunders. He's a fool, carving out disaster everywhere in his glaring need.

This cycle of hope and despair, desperation and disappointment, capped with humiliation and frustration, becomes so repetitive, invariable, that the note of inevitability creeps in. Maniacally manic, then grimly depressing in a total global gloom that cells him in to his dark doom of oneness.

Poor Al Lehman. He's mocked behind his back. Elbows poke neighbors' ribs, in a whispering conspiracy that confirms his laughing-stock reputation among those who see him everywhere they go as the stark figure of futility who stands out as a spurned nobody to everyone.

He's the obvious "no-one," the conspicuous nobody. How did he let himself get that way? He's going through a bad spell. He's starved for romance. His search for love seems almost deliberate as ineffectual motions he blindly goes through, depriving his deprivation-of-women of any hope for successful termination.

His pointed failures, his clownish gropings, his blunderbuss accostings, his fumbling overtures, his doomed-in-advance advances, his awkward attempts at smalltalk, chat; met always with rebuff, reproval, dismissal—they perpetuate themselves, proof upon proof that his methods, his manner, are self-defeating, deliberately so, leaving no detail unturned: masochism turned diabolically into refinement honed down to perfected degrees in the art of self-torture, the universal rejected buffoon of known and established identity, the well-recognised man-to-be-avoided, so clamoringly does he pant for ever-denied acceptance, respect, esteem, admiration, approval, acknowledgement of dignity.

A fool who can't stop trying. Trying *not* to be? Or trying *to* be? Either, or both.

He's just crashed a party. Gaiety, hilarity, loud chatter, clanking of ice cubes in intoxicating glasses. Music, noise everywhere. The din, prevailing.

He approaches a girl, a beautiful one, from the side. She does a little leap of surprise, detecting his sudden presence. "I've just been divorced, and lost my interim girlfriend, so you can imagine how lonely I am; no, how *can* you imagine it, if you've never experienced it?

"But force your compassion upon me. Love me, if only just a little. I implore you, to the begging of my bent knees. Have mercy. I adore you deeply. Have an affair with me, then let's get married. That alone could cure me of my chronic loneliness. Lend me your pity, your sympathy, your body, your all. I request no less. I want your whole soul."

"But I don't even *know* you."

"I'm Al Lehman."

"Ah, so *that's* who you are. The notorious Al Lehman? The failing beseecher of any woman's heart? So we've met at last. I've heard *so* much about you. You're spurned everywhere. The most rejected man-about-town. It's no wonder. Let me add *my* rejection, to all the others. A mere drop, in your aching oceanful of awful romantic agony."

Thus it goes. That illustrates what regularly happens to Al Lehman. A routine matter-of-course, at any party.

Luncheon parties, tea parties, cocktail parties, dinner parties, after-dinner parties, parties that include buffets or just drinks, art gallery openings, museum exhibit openings, film showings, theater previews—

Parties, parties, everywhere; but not a girl to kiss.

But not a love to win.

It's so awfully sad. His richly trembling soul, brimming over with loneliness, with lovelessness, an incurable everlasting ache from those honest Al Lehman depths. So sordid. So sublimely potential of great hunger, of joy, of feasts.

He can't do without people. He pursues them. They know it. They can do without him. That ardent man. Heaving wildly.

Built for love. But for another time, for another world. He missed that time, he missed that world. He's the crowned misfit of his uncooperative empire. His kingdom is in gay revolt. His subjects mock his rule. The women skirt free of his majestic impotence, while he stews in regal lust, and by his throne is an empty throne for a queen. No dainty mate will sit there. Not by *his* side. Not with *his* sterile crown. The uninvited king of parties. The lost guest. A guest lost, between parties. The least member of any gathering. In any secular congregation. The scorned lover of any woman. The last choice. He commands the greatest least. It's his, entering and departing. His lost social life is glittering everywhere. He circulates freely. Mobile, in any crowd.

Or mopes. Stared at. Studied, till pity's pain can't bear it.

And he wanders. Unclaimed. Longingly, but unbelongingly. The stranger, with so many stray homes.

Where people collect, romp together, disperse. Throngs or clusters, groups or mobs, occasions to get together. To meet in a casual setting, or formal; loose or mannered; evasive of commitment. Squadrons of introductions. All the formalities dispensed with. Short bits of chatter; prolonged discussions. Arrangements come to. Deals, connections, contacts, tentative agreements, flirtations, appointments, promises, exchange of address and telephone number, things worked out, in the making, broached, compromises, considerations. What goes on. Groping and clinches. Bouts of boredom, pulses of climax. Major events. Dull eventualities. Stray meetings, vital contacts. Random, or planned. Goings between. Doings on.

All-sized social events. Alike or dissimilar, functions or idlings. One shadow crosses them all: then blocked off, by shifting foreground bulk, regrouping.

One shadow flitters among them. Seen across a few years. He comes, he goes. Mostly he's always going. He's already leaving, as he enters. He crosses thresholds, opens doors, advances, departs.

His social motion is incessant. Here he is again. How nice to have him along. He joins our next party. It's all very harmonious. Hear him laughing. He's no longer lonely. A new girl likes him.

He's getting popular. We all like him. He's not the same. Nor are we. His lonely phase is over. He joins our human race again, he's all among us, we love him. He melts well in. He stands out well. His life likes him better. He's snapping out of the spell. He's become accepted. He's in a central flow. On the party-rotating world. In the swing of things. In the chic stream of swim. He's having a ball. In the global ballroom. He swirls round, hands out. And clutches love. O dear merry-go-round. How carnival you are. You blurred loneliness away. Now, people are delightful. We're all embraced. All in this round ride. To musical chimes, and roving color, and teeth of smiles, and love by bountifuls, in the encircling arms, that make a posey, and chain the world in flowers. Flowers that abound, sprung aloft, from man's sweet soil, from spring's human tide, from old earth, re-turned, till growth is tossed up. Men and women together. In the merry-go-clinch. All huddled up and hugged, all bundled up in tug-and-forth. Sailing on love's song, sails to the air. Flowers and music. Twined voices, caressed in a float. A throbbing circle of kisses. Our bodies meet, in soaring talk-cathedrals. We're all turned out, and into others. We change places. It's a peopled occasion. All this smothering chokes loneliness out: it drops away. It's lost.

No, loneliness is there. But it's lost its people. It can't find its people. It goes begging. The people are well lost. Loneliness looks among them, for them. But they're so close together, it can't find them. They're locked, enclosed, secure, from the isolation-monger.

Where's Al Lehman? He's all peopled over. He's all of them, and they him. He's so within. He's in among. He's joined on. He swings along.

Loneliness will never find him. Loneliness has lost him. It goes sobbing among the people, but can't locate him. He's in with everyone, but selectively. He's befriended and loved. Oh, such joy!

He's finally human. He's covered over, with the human. Overlaid. Deeply layered in.

Loneliness can't identify him. He goes unrecognised, to his own former self. He goes in, to his peopled heap. He soars out, on the swells of chorus. His own sound is there: unsingled-out, in vocal uttered collective all. A massive throat, quavering. Such universal combining. To drown out the separate persons. To clutter them over, in rich thick people. Shattering identity, in smooth sweepings. While outside, loneliness weeps: "Where are you, Al Lehman? I can't hear your own voice, which blends in to so many. We shared such pain together. We were shackled in chains of suffering. Now I'm lost, without you."

Loneliness creeps away. How can it be heard? In Al Lehman's ears, total sound is heard, slightly added to by his own voice, lost in the great human unison, a contribution that finds its home, that dwells within the grand old allness, a party that only existence is invited to on a shared basis, the party of our death, the life of our planet, the being in space, generations on a round gallop, the world's fair of time in the mind, of bodies in dusty continuity, of dear old duration, a strictly family affair.

Only members invited. Those who belong, arrive. Friendly doors are opened, to Al Lehman. On rounds of rides, in different forms of "along with," in the roar of open flux, surrounded by air and ocean, in the cosmopolitan context, on the wealthy earth with its door-to-door diversions in hospitality's current.

A nice group of people. To which add, "Al Lehman." Now they're all that much nicer. Love, friends, intimacy, acquaintance. All of Al Lehman is added in. His full functioning being. He's socially inside. He joins all that general soar. The roar of our music. That arranges silence and tames it harmless, finely patterned to harmony, even with a party at full blast, raging in din, curdled with hate, wild in sheer dissent, in open disorder, but formed along human lines, so we feel at home, all these combined guests, playing at host.

There's a moving light, from dark interlude to dark interlude. It puts other lights in the shade.

It's Al Lehman. Hello, Al. Now that *you're* here, so are we. That's our cue. We're the party, happily renewed. Let's go ahead. We're all here. The glasses are clean and empty, and our throats thirsty, but our hearts are full; so let's fill glasses and throats, and fill the space with love, exchanging talk all this while. For talk is our own sound. By it, we're here. Our attendance is marked, with notes of utterance. There are party wings, to wind our speech up, to all the song along, in the joined chorus. To heave our vocal power upon the voids before, the voids to come, in sheer might, in sheer fury, in all our orchestration, the boom we do, in our small sphere together.

XX. TWO STATES, DEPENDENTLY INDEPENDENT

Being drunk enough to want to do certain things that he was too drunk to do; being, because drunk, too lazy to do the things he was drunk enough to want to do; Al Lehman wondered: "How did I get this way? Was I drinking?" Shortly, the answer came from the same place of his wondering: "I was drinking. But is this me?"

Then he slept, and woke up sober. He was too sober to be drunk any more. He knew he *had* been drunk. But mainly, he knew that he knew that. "Here I am, being sober again," he had to confess. "I'm incurable. Again and again, I'm sober. I'll *never* break the habit. It must be, indeed, a deeply ingrained, deep-seated habit. Something impossible even to deal with, much less to get rid of."

With that, an inner peace settled in him. "Why fight it? Why fight my destiny? By *nature*, I'm sober. I submit. I accept. Sobriety is the true me. I must possess it, again and again. To weave in and out of drunkenness, to become sober anew, again and again. To repeat it. Having lost it. Having been drunk enough, to resume being sober. All over."

This was the pattern he cut out for himself. In alternating currents. Like night, day, night, day. To be drunk enough, and then be sober. In contrast, by repetition.

It takes one, to know the other.

He's sober now. He knows it, how? He had been drunk. And starts again.

XXI.

(Title isn't here. It comes, rather, as an afterpiece. So go straight to the text:)

Waking from an alcoholic stupor, Al Lehman wondered just where he was. "Right here," a voice told him.

"How right you are," Al Lehman replied. "But who—if I may so ask—are you?"

"Oh, just a voice," the voice demurely declared.

"A bodiless one?" Al Lehman found fit to ask.

"Yes. I'm a voice without a body. I'm *looking* for a body to contain me. Perhaps someone with laryngitis would take me in for a while, for a temporary home. I'm a wandering waif of a vagrant, a bodiless voice, haunting other people's ears."

"Are *you* a person?" Al Lehman asked.

"I'm not complete enough to be one—I'm only a voice."

"That's certainly not enough to be a well-rounded person. You sure are lacking!"

"I'm lacking a body to be in. I'll search the most remote corners of heaven and earth, till I find one."

"Do you prefer a *man's* body for your living quarters?"

"Yes."

"Why is that?"

"I'm attracted to women."

"That's quite masculine of you."

"It is."

"You're more of a tenor than a baritone."

"Yes, but Caruso would have rejected me."

"I can see why: you're quite unoperatic."

"Yet, in a way, I *can* operate."

"Yes, you *can* operate. Maybe you should be in a *surgeon's* body."

"No, for then my tones would be sharp and cutting. I just wasn't chiseled out for that sort of thing."

"Whose body would you like to habitate?"

"That of a folk singer."

"Then you entertain musical ambitions?"

"No, but I'm the potential instrument for a body whose owner *does* entertain singing ambitions."

"How will you go about gaining residence in such a body?"

"It wouldn't be easy; for I'd have to displace that body's *own* current voice, which has long and habitually resided there as 'a part of the family,' so to speak."

"I pity you, poor voice. *Do* gain a home."

"Could *you*, Al Lehman, put me up?"

"Sorry. I already *have* a voice. In fact, I've been speaking to you with it."

"So I've been hearing. You call it a voice?"

"It's tuneful and melodious. I wouldn't exchange it for you, dear voice. Nor would I take you in, and harbor two voices simultaneously; for that would confuse my integrated unity."

"Couldn't you *assimilate* me to your integrated unity?—I promise not to be out of tune with your old habitual voice."

"No. One's enough. Goodbye."

"You're silencing me?"

"Not by walking away from you, which I intend to do. I'll be out of hearing range from you. Talk on, dear voice; but to *me* no longer."

"You'll stop listening, by leaving?"

"Yes, voice. I'm tired of you."

"I'll haunt someone *else's* ear, now; since you've tired of me."

"Thank you. I crave silence. I gain it by walking away from you. May you as easily gain the body you crave to be in—ideally, preferably, one with folk-singing ambitions, and the talent to use, refine, develop, the tuneful potentialities in your tone."

"Thank you, Al Lehman. . . He's gone. I'm alone. He was drunk, so I found him easy to talk to. Then, gradually, he became sober. That caused me to lose him as a listener. I'll wander to a party or a bar, where someone else will be drunk enough for me to haunt him. Ideally, preferably, a would-be folksinger who's lost his voice. Which I'd replace. And, in time, *dis*place. Then *that* voice need never be found. And I'd gain a home, forever."

(Title as afterpiece:)

ANY BODY NEED A VOICE? IF YOU'RE A FOLKSINGER, THERE'S A VOICE THAT'S INTERESTED IN FINDING A HOME IN YOU. IT HAS NO BODY OF ITS OWN. BUT FIRST, LOSE YOUR OWN, OLD VOICE. THEN THIS ONE WOULD SEEK TO REPLACE IT, PERMANENTLY. IT HAS VERY "SOUND" CREDENTIALS. GIVE IT, AT LEAST, A HEARING.

XXII. DRUNKENNESS AND AFTERWARD

"You're drunk enough to be too lazy to do what you're drunk enough to want to do," observed a friend, Murray, to Al Lehman, who exactly fit that uncomplimentary description, even down to certain hazy details, which, though vivid to Murray, were lost on Al Lehman in his present condition.

He gamely tried to make coherent sense in conversation. "What's that, Murray? Drunkenness makes me want to do what I'm too drunk to have the energy for doing?"

"You twisted it, Al. But you've grasped the drift, in some slant."

"Good. Sober me up, will you? Where's the party? It's not going on any more."

"It's over. The guests have gone home. All but you. You're in no fit condition to go home. So I'm putting you up here for the night, in my guest room. Just sleep it off, and you'll be recovered by the morning."

"That's kind of you. Were you the party host?"

"Sure. It's the same apartment now, as the one where the party has just recently ended. It's where I still live, in both states: party host, and your private host."

"What did I want to do in drunken craving that I was too drunk to carry out?"

"To fight someone and to fornicate with someone else. They both dismissed you, from your feeble overtures."

"How disgraceful. Did I look foolish?"

"Enough to be laughed at."

"What else did I ineffectually muddle at, in stupor?"

"You tried to explain something to an intellectual, but merely babbled. You also tried to eat, but spilled the food.

You began things, went through motions, but couldn't carry them through. You were left hanging, from your own projects, attempt after abortive attempt, snuffed out in the drowse of inertia."

"Was I uncoordinated, incoherent, fumbling, disjointed, not of a piece?"

"All those, in classic drunken syndrome."

"I'm disgusted. I repent."

"No-one cared. You were amusing."

"But my dignity failed. My esteem is lowered, with those people. And my fun was only 'unconscious.' I regret all that I did—or rather, didn't do, so ingloriously."

"You lost a little pride and vanity. But people made allowances for the drunken circumstances. Your credit is still good, on past character performance."

"Which I proceeded to degrade."

"But not destroy. Go easy on drink, next party: you'll redeem yourself."

"Thanks for your description and encouragement. You're a good friend, Murray. You're good to me. Now, I'll fall asleep."

"Your drunkenness is wearing off. You're making sense. You still have enough drunkenness left, to achieve good success in going to sleep. Use it."

"Thanks, Murray. Good sleep to *you*, too."

"But not yet."

"Why? What's first?"

"Margaret is in my bed. You weren't *really* the only remaining guest. She'll honor me by staying, too: but more actively."

"With you? But I was trying to seduce her all night!"

"You might have, but were too drunk. Your failure became, then, my opportunity."

Murray closed the door behind him, bouncing off to some pleasure. Al Lehman brooded jealously. It slightly soiled his recent gratitude.

Well, if *he* couldn't have her, at least she'll make *Murray* happy, who now extends party hospitality to an exclusive amorous conclusion, in that private party of completely two.

Al Lehman was asleep. In another room, Murray and Margaret were hardly that. They were doing what Margaret might be doing, now, instead, with Al Lehman, in her or his apartment, had only he not lost out by losing his hold, dropping contact, in alcoholic blur, which can barely support just one solitude, despite such terrible overtures to the contrary, such violent intentions, such frenzied behavior. Alone. In transitional oblivion. Toward a restored social will, in good sober force, tomorrow.

XXIII. IF SUPPLICATION PAYS OFF, AND WE'RE PLACED BEYOND THE NEED TO PRAY OR PLACATE, ENJOYING "FATE"'S FOND FAVOR, IS PRAISE STILL OWED TO CREDIT THE AGENCY PREVIOUSLY PRAYED TO WHEN PERILOUS CRISIS MADE US CRAVEN PETITIONERS? OR IS THE DEBT CANCELED, NOW THAT WE CAN DISDAIN THE DESPERATE MAGIC OF SOME IMPLORED AID?

Al Lehman was in a disaster, which threatened to become catastrophic, and wreak utter devastation, all-consuming annihilation, upon his entire life and all the rest of it. In this emergency, he had to act quickly. Yes, but how?

How, indeed, might he extricate himself—unscathed or with minimum damage—from this crucially critical, critically crucial crisis?—aye, that's the crux.

By himself alone, he was all but helpless. Appeal, then, would have to be made. To what higher authority, to dispense intervention? Al Lehman's will was ineffectually puny for stemming the overwhelming tides of external indifference, cold cosmic disdain, for his punily ineffectual will that now desperately besought, in utter extremity and dire perplexity in grim malevolence of plight, a spot of timely assistance from the Almighty, some magic or unnatural miracle that would work wonders to change circumstances and frame the situation to forge a blessing in grace and favor to promote better conditions and secure a greater advantage, reverse misfortune till suns smile on brighter prospects and sweet endeavor and lighten Al Lehman's lot.

God's skillful mercy should suffice to turn this tricky deal from peril to peace, a chemical good from the base metallic bad.

Pious prayer, to placate or supplicate such power on behalf of the petitioner who submits his meekness to the awesomeness humbly solicited, is gravely resorted to.

The crisis evaporates. The catastrophe never occurs. The devastation never devastated. The crucial annihilation didn't take place.

Danger has fled. Peril has perished. Hazard is a has-been. A safe situation is retrieved. A new, harmless set of circumstances has appeared. Did prayer turn the trick? Did God's skillful mercy intervene with blessing, grace, and favor, destroying bad conditions and promoting benevolent factors?

Or would good fortune have come without divine magic? Al Lehman's problem, now that his personal prospects are pleasing, is a matter of gratitude. Is gratitude due? Who gets the credit? He's out of trouble. Would the sun have smiled on him *anyway*, without prayer? Is thanks owing to God? *Is* there a God? Now that none is needed?

XXIV. LIFE THROUGH THE WINDOW-PAIN

The martyr to pain-avoidance. That's what poor Al Lehman has become. He takes more pains to avoid pain than the avoidance of pain in the first place is worth. He's painstakingly careful to get out of pain's way. Plainly, it's all one big pain, to him.

XXV. WHAT AL LEHMAN WOULD DO, JUST TO AVOID PAIN

Pain is a great guide of what to avoid, Al Lehman found out. To follow pain's self-ridding advice became wisdom's keystone or foundation. Now, Al Lehman can't do without the doing-without of pain, which he leaves in the lurch whenever he can, through one great dodge or another.

His pain-aversion has amounted to an art. He tries to give pain the slip, to steer a wide berth around its clamorous closing-in.

Physical pain, he deplores. Suffering, worry, sorrow, anxiety, discomfort, grief, anguish, terror, and misery are also low on his list of priorities to be valued.

His detestation of pain reaches extremes. He takes terrible pains just to avoid pain. He goes to great lengths. He agonizes, excruciatingly, over the slightest pain, the most minor irritation. He lavishes painstaking remedies, he elaborates meticulous care, in applying ruthless pain-relievings, to deter the least distress. He vastly troubles over what's not worth all that trouble. He goes through such a bother over mere trifles. He's committed, with zeal and devotion, to these rigorous tasks. He takes incredible pains over them. He simply goes through hell.

Oh, the hell he goes through! And why? Because he finds pain unbearable. Why, he'll go through hell, just to avoid pain.

He simply can't endure pain. He has the lowest threshold of tolerance for it. He'd do *anything*, to avoid it!

He's a martyr to the avoidance of pain. He burns at the stake, of his own stubborn martyrdom.

But it's *worth* all those pains. He's put himself to the rack, he's ruined himself, but he's stuck to it! He could take it! And come back, for more. He's a glutton, for it. He can't get enough of it. His nerves are battered, his health is shattered; but he hurls himself, once more, back to the front, and takes it in the teeth. Still, he comes back for more.

He asks for punishment, he's indomitable, a fortress under siege.

Oh, we must cover our eyes with our hands! We can't bear to see it, any more. It's beyond endurance.

XXVI. FAILING TO INVENT OR DISCOVER A NEW DIMENSION TO GO ALONG WITH TIME AND SPACE, AL LEHMAN CHATS WITH GOD, WHO'S ALSO BEEN STRIPPED OF ALL BUT HIS NAME, IN THE REVERSALS AND SETBACKS HE'S SUFFERED AT THE SKEPTICAL HANDS OF THE WORLD'S BANAL LITERALNESS THAT CHOKES OFF ALL ACCESS TO DIVINELY RADIANT HORIZONS THAT HURL TRUTH FORTH ON BEAMS OF MYSTERY.

Al Lehman was looking for a new dimension. A few were "all sewed up," the market cornered, by prior discoverers or inventors.

(The ultimate in discovery and the ultimate in invention are approximately the same. What's discoverable and what's inventable are unlimited in the same limited direction. But anyway, back to Al Lehman.)

It was too late for Al Lehman to discover (or invent) Time. Time has been going on for a long time. It means to stay that way, and keep on going on, if it has anything to say about it, if it can at all help it.

It has two things going for it: duration, and successiveness. With those stock capital assets of basic mobile durability, Time, which is essentially temporal, is going to hang around for a long time. The world would be cutting off its own nose if it attempted to get rid of it.

And why would the world, anyway, want to do away with time? Time is a valuable ally to any worldly process, whatever. Without time, everything would always be happening at once. That's much too simultaneous for our own comfort or convenience.

Time manages to keep events apart, so each gets its proper due of attention. It retards some things till previous things can undergo their full extent. It exercises a delaying effect, to separate our human experiences into digestible, reflected-upon units, so we can size things up and plan ahead, utilizing our recent learnings for our later reckonings and calculations.

Time has already been invented or discovered, and worked over, even formulated; it's been made a definite point of.

Spatial dimensions have pretty well been charted, as well. The front-back plane; the left-right plane; the up-down plane: we're all thoroughly familiar with them, from any angle. Visual experiences have been voluminously commonplace, and obvious to a mysterious degree.

So what remained for Al Lehman to invent or discover, in the realm of dimensionality (if there *is* such a realm; if not, let's assume it), that hasn't already been co-opted to human use?

Al Lehman didn't want to be an anonymous nonentity. He wanted to be notable (a word sharing its root with note or notice). He wanted, in short, to make his mark.

The human race had done, thank you, quite nicely without Al Lehman's assistance. Well, how could he change that?

To try to claim the invention or discovery by his own personal research of space or time (or, for that matter, both) would be like trying to sell an institution like the Brooklyn Bridge or the Grand Canyon to a naive sucker, an Indian who doesn't know any better, or a fool on whom a confidence trick may be worked.

But Al Lehman yearned to discover or invent something precious, worthy, valuable, momentous, or significant. That would make his name, put him on the map, and guarantee his fame.

Easier, of course, said than done; easier thought and dreamed as a grandiose scheme of air, than actually brought into achievement.

He pondered. What heroic conquest could he make of an as-yet-unearthed mystery? What daring, inspired solution to what vast problem?f What was the universe short of, but had need for, in that special sphere of new knowledge?

He was at a loss. He faced, alas, defeat.

Failure to contribute to mankind's global self-knowledge stared him, blankly, in the face. Was he only a consumer of what *others* had invented or discovered?' Had he no active role in extending the bold boundary, the evolutionary current, of universally significant truth?

He would just re-use what was already in motion? And add not one log to revelation's great bonfire?

Such seemed his dismal case. He smarted, to fall deficient, when those before him, and after him, kindled sparks of light to set back stark darkness to grant a cautious gain for our collective mentality.

Time and space are already ours. The borders of matter have been thoroughly explored. The elements had become our common alphabet.

The spiritual dimension, as an abstraction, isolated from all the rest, is nonexistent. He wouldn't resort to mystic fakery.

Our ignorance is lined with knowledge. We're well padded, behind protective layers of known, accepted things, given and granted.

Yet, still mystery lurks. What's missing? That's the key.

Thought was to no avail. Al Lehman stopped such strenuous futility.

Mankind had nothing to thank him for. No wonder he went unnoticed.

Still, he searches. But for what?

A dimension overlooked till now. Which, when found, or created (discovered or invented), would change everything we now knew. Would bound us, in a new whole.

What vital part, what intrinsic link, remains unspoken for?

Transformed into a hero with laurels of genius, Al Lehman would shed brilliant light on the immense totality of the whole All, which seems to have everything, except some something. What is, perhaps, that little something? Which, when known, would alter this huge All?

"Help me, God. I look in vain."

"For what, Al Lehman?"

"How do *I* know? I haven't found it."

"Then why not invent it?"

"I need your guidance."

"What do you expect? I'm only God."

"*Only*!? That's *plenty.*"

"In today's world, I'm merely finite. I'm not much believed in these days."

"I'll make a pact with you. I'll help improve your credibility, if you inspire me with divine light."

"Sorry. I'm not corruptible by bribe. I'm *God*, you realize. Stop bargaining with me as though I weren't."

"You're quite pure?"

"I always was."

"I want to make a major discovery—or invention—to make the world literally sit up and take notice. To give my vanity great fame in my small lifetime."

"Well, what's stopping you?"

"Ignorance. Dullness. Obscurity. The lack of light."

"Are you asking me. . ."

"I'm *praying*."

"Sorry. Live by your own lights. I'm not what once I was reputed to be. My power's been curtailed."

"Am I doggedly barking up, then, the wrong tree?"

"So it seems, to me."

"Can you grant me *any* clue, or advice?"

"That's like asking a bum for a handout. I'm in the dark, myself."

"Then are you any sort of God at all?"

"Effectually, no. Nominally, yes. I'm down-at-heels, seedy and shabby, a ghost of my former great Name. All I have is a former reputation, trumped-up, a hollow mockery of all that had been claimed for my Omnipresent Rule, my divine Omniscience. I'm but the shell, whose vital inside has escaped, the organic core quite quelled."'

"What a beggar! You make yourself ignobly transparent. Can't pride at least put on a front?"

"My vanity has nothing to hold it up. It's collapsed, in a heap."

"Well, *you*'re my discovery. I'll take credit, for inventing Your demise."

"That's old-hat. My demise is nothing new, by now. You haven't made any theological breakthrough by recognizing how fallen I am."

"Is there *one* gift of knowledge I can bestow on mankind?—or particle, or portion, of such?"

"Everything's been covered. You're too late."

"Damn you, then!"

"I already am."

"Then let me out of here. Where are we talking?"

"In 'heaven.' "

"But am I dead?"

"No. Just visiting."

"Thank God. I must return."

"Empty-handed, I'm afraid."

"Yes. Thanks for nothing."

"That's all I have. Nothing: and plenty of it."

"For my purposes, that's not sufficiently substantial."

"Well, it'll have to do. It's the only substitute there is, negatively speaking, for everything else."

"You're no help. Thanks for nothing."

"Take *plenty* of it—all you need."

"A *little* nothing will do. More is just so much of the same."

"Go back to time and space."

"I don't feel at home *there,* either."

"Then you're a lost soul."

"So you've found me to be."

"You're that without the need of my finding it so. There's nothing *official* to it: you're just lost."

"I crave to be found. Constituted. Determined. Established. Confirmed."

"You're *already* Al Lehman. Has that no substance?"

"I haven't *done* anything; *achieved* anything; *made* anything; *acquired* anything. I'm not complete, I'm barely begun."

"Go back, see what you can finish. Take on modest goals, as fitting your narrow scope. Do *something*, at least."

"There's some small hope in that."

"Flee. I'm dead."

"Thanks, God. You're a ghost of your former self. All your magic has been squeezed out. Still, I can name-drop you, now, upon my social return to the world's snob-hierarchy of gossip and reputation, of rank and profession. There's still some worth, in your old name. It could conjure up a potent spell or two. It won't dent the time-space complex; but it *will* impress, as snob-appeal. I'll rise in social standing. Thanks."

"Your name is vanity."

"Just call me Al, Your Highness."

"Address me as God. In these deflated heavens, that's all I have—my Holy Name."

Al Lehman is back in time and space. He feels as though he never left that old cold home of his. Maybe, all this time, he's still been there. Carrying on a self-dialogue, deluded in some divine mirage partner.

He plods along. In the curse of the familiar. By dim dull light of days ordinary and plain. Without guidance. Missing what's central. Possessing no key unknown, which, were he to possess it, would match up his earth with the precise heaven it needs. That one heaven he always lacks. Leaving earth flat. Grim time. Dull space. Nothing else. A toy cosmos. Deprived of its own depth. Rich in the broken promise of the lack he'll never provide. In his level of routine light. Moved to mechanical time. Freely hemmed in to the ample prison of space.

To break loose is his dying wish. To break bounds. To be made, by some sharp break.

No God to guide him. Locked up in the dimensions provided for him. Al Lehman. The lost seeker. The non-inventor. Still missing his self-finding discovery.

He's endured truth too long. He needs to put the lie to it. For another truth would lie in wait: the truth that's not yet. That shakes his parts loose, and snaps them to a different order. Introducing the next unity. An all-solving form. A supernatural departure, to open up greater clarity upon the obvious.

He fails, having died. But he was close.

It was inside him, all the while. The world in a wild state. He couldn't find it. He was too tame. The world looked the same. It stayed put. Knowledge was kept domestic to custom's stale use, by which the recognized world retained its sterility. There was the stable view. It repeated the old dimensions. Obedience was well rehearsed. The mind was a trained machine. It released no Idea.

It was *there*, but not seen. It was in on Al Lehman. The invention or discovery not made. The bland world, clad in the well known. What everyone accepts.

Al Lehman was unhappy. He couldn't accept what was. He longed for what it was not. He came up empty.

There *is* a furious fullness. But where?

It's too glaring. But it's there.

It's too much there. Thought can't center on it. Thought travels everywhere else. Everywhere, but There, and never just when the When is There. Thought lacks that sole contact. Its pure hole.

XXVII. AL LEHMAN'S MANHOOD GETS DISVANI-TIED.

A girl said yes, so Al Lehman set upon her with the full enormity of his beast driven furiously to lust.

Yet, when he was finished, he saw that he'd barely made a dent upon her.

She rose unperturbed, untumbled, untarnished, unflapped, unruffled.

"Is *that* all the effect I've had upon you?" he asked.

To which she replied, "Oh, was it you? Sorry, my eyes were closed. I thought my pet kitten was scampering over my lap on its light little toes."

"Was *that* all my manhood did to you!?" Al Lehman, dismayed, cried.

She nodded gaily. Men were so vain. Her job was to disvanity them. Where better, than at their vulnerable seats of sheer manhood's colossal vanity?

Poor Al Lehman wept. The girl was lighthearted. In glee, she danced, with her sly mocking.

XXVIII. WHAT A WAY TO LOSE A JOB! AND MISS THE CONSOLATION, AS WELL.

Every time Harriet wriggled past him, in the office, distracted Al Lehman from his desk-work. He was being closely monitored, on the job. The new company policy from the higher-ups was to reduce the staff in the economic cut-back, in order financially to survive. Salaries were frozen at the present level. In addition, half the employees would have to be let go. Al Lehman's job was in dire jeopardy. He resolved to work at an extraordinary pace, to get mounds of work done at high calibers of excellence, so as to create an impression of overwhelming competence on the office manager, department supervisor, and vice-presidential executives who were hawkishly noseying about to detect flaws and performance failures to justify the firings they, like hangmen, had been given the solemn office of executing, hence their rank, "executives," for they can coldly kill eager career hopes, intense professional ambitions, with a chilling impersonality and god-like detachment of dispatch.

Al Lehman was fighting to retain his job. He arrived early, remained late, bent down in devout concentration on his sacred desk papers.

For all his determination, he found himself distracted by Harriet, wriggling by. She was a shapely secretary whose job was secure. Hers was one of the eight desks in the office Al Lehman shared. She could type rapidly and accurately on her stream-lined machine that bolted upright on her desk. To look at, she was gorgeous. Al Lehman cast looks upon her. These looks could be fatal. They sapped his concentration on work. He had, by main effort of force and will, to plunge himself back into business matters. But then she'd wriggle by again: his grasp on work would weaken. She was slowly costing him his job. Office manager, department supervisor, vice-presidential executives in charge of discharge, noticed his slackening of attention. They smiled, detecting Harriet's body for the cause.

Finally, Al Lehman was given his notice. Despite the long hours he put in every day, his efficiency production output had fallen below required standards. The company no longer needed his services. He was fired, as of next Monday. The firm had been firm with him. He was finished. Other firms in allied fields, due to an economic recession that created hordes of unemployed, just were not hiring. Al Lehman would be out of work, without good prospects. His career in this chosen field was perhaps good and dead. His record would be held against him, with other firms, even on economic recovery: he had been ousted from his post in disgrace of being fired. His ambitions might never recover, from such lethal assessment of his commercial ability by a firm whose judgments were highly held in that competitive trade.

"Harriet, why did you wriggle past me all the time like that? See what it's done? Why did you walk enticingly by *my* desk, at the peak of my concentration? Couldn't you have been more inconspicuous, and chosen other routes that less diverted my attention? My wife Marge, with whom I'm on near-divorce terms, will hold my firing against me, to her advantage, in our incessant 'power' struggle of incompatible wills. My son Gregory— how can I afford, when the time comes years hence, to put him through college? My life is ruined: due to you."

"Don't be too harsh on me, Al Lehman. I *had* to do it."

" '*Had to,*' Harriet? You *had to* get me fired, by your seductive weakening of my concentration during key office hours? Is that a confession? But why?"

"I had to, because your direct rival for retention of identical posts which the management had decided to reduce to one, measuring you in competition against him for that sole position, is Bob, whom I love. My chances of marrying him would be lost were he to lose that job. Thus, I sabotaged you, his sole rival, by lowering your work performance efficiency production output results quota by swaying my lovely body regularly in the way of your lust-lost eyes. It worked, perfectly. You're fired, Bob's job is safe and secure, and he and I will soon marry. I'm grateful to your weakness, which is sex, for the fulfillment of my love in the happy promise of domestic bliss. We want to invite you to our wedding. Without your optical seductibility, our romance would have died an ugly commercial death of thwarted ambition, the loss of professional status, the ruin of a promising career. Now, Bob is blooming, thanks to you. His future gleams with glorious promise. How sad, that your downfall was the necessary condition for *our* bright secure prosperity and marital blessing. It was either you or us. Sorry."

What could Al Lehman say? He was speechless. She had brought him down, with low tactics—aiming at his signal weakness below the belt. All, though, is fair, in love, and business— which is the peacetime equivalent of war.

Fallen was Al Lehman. The times were bad. He's become a casualty of them.

He turned down Harriet's wedding invitation. He envied Bob, who'd have—and had already—the freedom to pit his lust against her lovely body. How Al Lehman preferred her, to Marge! Bob had the woman he lusted for, and his job as well.

Bob avoided Al Lehman. Friday came—Al's last day at that firm, forever. He exchanged farewells with all his former colleagues. Some of them would soon lose *their* jobs, as well. Throughout the offices, tears could be spotted.

Bob was out sick that day. Harriet looked luscious, in a see-through dress that added to poor Al Lehman's already over-wrought torments.

She wriggled over to him. "You can make love to me, if you wish, after work, today. Bob need never know. It's my recompense, or reparation, for what I've done to you. You can take your frustrating disappointment out on my gripping body. I owe it to you. I brought you low."

"You did, Harriet. I'll take you up, on your ethically ambivalent offer."

They went to a cheap hotel room, after work. Bob was in Harriet's apartment, Marge and Gregory in Al's. So they purchased a sort of dingy privacy, in a hotel.

It was a squalid affair. Al couldn't "do" it. He was impotent. Harriet smiled, with contempt. Here was his chance for some slight consolation, all condensed in anguished brevity. He failed.

"You're fired," Harriet teased him. "You bungled *this* job, too. Your impotence is of course situational. You're too miserable to perform. It's enabled me to remain faithful to my dear Bob. He has both me, and your job. Both of which, *you*'d like, wouldn't you?"

She dressed and left, while Al Lehman sobbed. His life had sunk very low. He had, in fact, touched the murky bottom of his depths of misfortune. It would be a long reversal, till he surfaces once more. His future offered only the prospect of change. To that, his faint hopes clung. Endure this "now." He was undressed, in a dingy bed. Without job, soon without wife. Harriet was gone. Now, he felt lust. Too late.

XXIX. GLORIA'S LEGS IN AN ADMIRER'S HEAD, BUT GLORIA GRABS THEM BACK AGAIN, AS HER OWN BELONGINGS, NOT PLUNDERABLE BY AN ALIEN SNATCHER ACROSS INVIOLATE BOUNDARIES ESTABLISHED BY PERSONAL LAW, THE BORDER SANCTITY OF THE BODY POLITIC'S INALIENABLE AUTONOMY, EVEN TO THE UTMOST EXTREMITIES OF THE VERY LEGS THAT FASCINATE THE FOREIGN NEIGHBOR.

Al Lehman's desk was on the eleventh floor. Across the aisle or corridor was an opposite row of desks, filing cabinets, and other office essentials. Along that row, to the right, was a desk occupied by Gloria, whose face was seen behind a large, ornate, black, old typewriter.

Well, what about her? Al Lehman was in love with her. That's how important she was to him.

He was a lonely young bachelor, in those remote days before he met and married Marge who bore him their son Gregory.

The legs of Gloria's desk infuriated Al Lehman, for obscuring the more desirable-to-be-seen pair of human legs, the wooden blocking off the fleshy ones.

Such obstruction kindled Al Lehman to compensation-by-imagination. He reconstructed so often Gloria's physically hidden legs, that the desk was well-nigh worn out by the visually lusty mentality of a voyeur cheated in his direct quest for sight, turned visionary in vision's deprivation. Gloria's legs knew nothing of this. Why should they, with Gloria herself in the dark, as her lower possessions were in the dark about their being a matter of illumination to their frustrated watcher's wild mind churning out gorgeous images in the radiant loneliness of his deprived sight.

But Gloria would get up and walk, too: this or that way, or else, usually, some other way.

Given a clear view, Al Lehman didn't discard his images, but twisted them into suitable harmony with what he was now privileged to witness.

Never were her legs entirely free of the mental additions, augmenting them, which Al Lehman took the liberty of imposing upon them: gifted imagination's licentious license to exalt the gifted pair of subject legs under intense scrutiny, close study, devout contemplation; rapt holy steady absorption, fanatic, mad, poetic, zealous; obsession that alters the object which inspires it: converting concrete tangibles

(the curvature interplay of shins flowing into ankles, knees swollen into calves, thighs bursting into broad buttocks and groaning groin behind the skirt's tasselled drapery tossed in folds and flung, jigged about, like curtains that dance and bend to the open window's light incoming blast of breeze variations),

converting concrete tangibles into ideal spiritual essence, the organic play of pure mentality, the lower forms of higher love, sublime translations of carnal substance in the dancing realm of God's holy lust.

Thus, Al Lehman broke the unity, cracked the continuity, of Gloria and her own legs. His own world colonized the breach.

Her legs spoke to him. He picked up on that. He compiled a whole grammar to give a body and form to his listening.

Her legs articulated themselves, while Al Lehman turned linguist to this lovely new language, the language of Gloria's legs, their syntax, nouns, verbs, adverbs, adjectives, conjunctives, pronouns, the murmuring vocabulary, the declensions and inflections, colloquial and formal, corruptions and pedan-tic inbredness, the prosody, poetics, and terminology of that oc-cult tongue.

Gloria was in the dark, as were her legs, as to the cult the latter were being made by the private worshipper.

Gloria did her paperwork, Al did his; they belonged to overlapping departments of the commercial unit of the service branch of the publicity division of the advertising bureau of the industrial section of the communications building of their business firm in whose joint employ they found themselves through obliquely facing desks in the same room droning with account manipulation and clerical tabulation, the filling and sorting of forms, processing of records through which the orga-nization kept prolonging itself and notified the public of all the forced benefits thus offered.

In those days, Al Lehman was living with his mother and stepfather. He'd toss in bed at night, stirred by curving angles and glimpses by varied projectories of those stunning under-pinnings with which Gloria did all her graceful walking and other maneuvers requiring the posture that sprang from the ground, the twin roots that branched into one torso, revers-ing the trunk division of every tree known to darkened glades or bright residential community. No-one in his right eyesight would confuse Gloria's lower limbs with any tree's delicately sculpted trunk. Al Lehman made a clear distinction, at those points.

Further yet, he distinguished Gloria's legs from those of any other member of her gender or even species, the earth-swarming tribe of humankind, evolution's latest success story.

He squirmed in bed at night, in the house of his mother and stepfather, seeing pose and hose of unsuspecting Gloria's stable supports.

He split Gloria from her legs. Instead of being in love with the whole unit, the total ensemble from head to fingertip to toe of the organic organism in question, he decided to specialize his love in the legs themselves. To hell with the northern remnants that remained attached to the lovely focal objects of his devotion. He narrowed down his sacred idolatry field. Such particularity sharpened his concentration along lines sublimely delineated, and harnessed his orientation to his superb specialty.

As to Gloria herself, naturally enough she'd never agree to his brutal schism, this bodily divorce of herself, designated by the beau of her lower parts. She would insist on her own perfect unity, a federal government that has voided the secession of southern members but whose crowned wholeness concedes states' rights to neutralize the despotic potential of central rule.

How, then, to single out the legs themselves as a self-determined separate autonomy? Bodily integrity would confiscate by interception a love-missive directed to the legs alone.

It was nearly the Christmas season, when the spirit of giving generously materialized itself in gifts.

Al Lehman would give a present to the legs of Gloria, addressed to those legs, as carefully demarcated, cut off from the woman's extraneous upper aspects.

But she'd act as a whole, and claim the gift for all of herself. Al Lehman's course of specified love foresaw that gross obstacle.

The obstruction by the whole would deny Al Lehman the particularity of his chosen parts. The road of love grew bumpy, and no smooth sailing was ahead.

This problem knotted Al Lehman to insoluble pondering. Nor could precedence afford him the legacy of a previous solution.

He hated the rest of Gloria, for its gross interference; its cynical disruption of true love.

His love, alas, was on its last legs. How could it sturdily uphold itself, to quell the rioting on top?

He sent to the loved legs a pair of stockings for a Christmas gift, but *all* of Gloria assimilated it, though only her legs themselves could wear it.

The donor's name, "Al Lehman," rested on the package. In the corridor of their office room, they spoke. "It was intended for them?", she pointed to her lower parts.

"Strictly," Al Lehman assured her.

"I'm one unit, or nothing. I spurn your gift, then. Here it is, returned."

"You speak on *behalf* of them?"

"I'm their fledged representative, and we're all in this together," she motioned, caressing her whole body at once, in a sweeping gesture all-inclusive, under the sway of her central ego that surveyed the whole. "*We*'re returning this to you. We find it unacceptable."

The pair of stockings was handed over, in its package. "Then I'll marry your entire Communist nation," offered Al Lehman, as he widened the scope of his love to all of Gloria's approved northern boundaries, encompassing the body politic of even her outmost extremities in any indicated direction of the territorial prerogative exercised by the emancipated republic of her nationhood, her geographically manifested nationalism to the height and breadth and width of the global borders allotted, within the flag and dominion of her central government to the proud unfurling of extended limits as provided by charter.

"Sorry, I'm engaged," she replied, denying him access to legs and all the rest.

Al Lehman requested that his desk be moved to a remote end of the office, out of sight of Gloria, legs and all, to a site recently vacated by a retired worker. This was granted.

But she passes by, or he passes by, but he avoids her eye, when inadvertently they do meet.

The winking eyes of her knees, he never dares look down to.

His leg-imagery has been suppressed. It was unmanageably cluttered. It went weedy, with Gloria's interference.

XXX. TRUTH, THE ELEPHANT THAT TRAMPLES ON PEOPLE'S VANITY-TOES. SHOULD IT GO WILD, OR BE CURBED? LET LOOSE ON A BLUNT AWKWARD RAMPAGE; OR DECKED OUT IN MINCED DELICACY AND LED MOST DECOROUSLY ALONG, NEVER STOMPING ON THE PRECIOUS TOES OF PEOPLE'S TRUTH-REBUTTALED DIGNITY?

"Truth is an elephant that, let loose to blunder about wildly in its random shuffle or rumble, is bound, somehow or other, to trample on some people's favorite vanity toes."

That was Al Lehman's explanation or excuse to a hostess he had severely insulted, or given offense to, inadvertently, by saying something true which too intimately applied to her in a most unflattering way.

"Leave," she directed, motioning to the door. He did as told, but quick. The other guests smirked, or so he thought, as they snugly remained, as Al Lehman was expelled in disgrace from a gathering he was so embarrassed to leave by way of that openly humiliating directive by the haughty hostess whose precious square of dignity he had truthfully blundered against in his honest open offensive candor of trampling on her delicate vanity toes with his blunt elephantine shuffle that roams coarsely about in the awkward heavy shelter of homely truth on a rampage, truth too bare for socializing cosmetics to hone down and temper to a tone of civility.

The outcast guest, head hanging down, wends his way homeward with slow, deliberate steps. "Cosmetic doctoring of anti-social truth compromises truth in order not to compromise people's precious reputation. Truth has to be dressed up in self-disguise, so as not to be vanity's most dangerous enemy.

I'm caught in a quagmire. Must I keep the truth unexpressed in order to be socially acceptable? Selective truth is truth falsified. Unexpressed truth is truth undeveloped. Omitted truth is truth aborted. Truth decorously decked out is truth debased of its very name.

"But I want—need—to get along well with people sensitive for their vain reputations. But not to the cost of the truth, at sacrifice of veracity. Thus, the quagmire I'm in. I sink and soar, and tug, at wrestle with this dilemma. I want an approved social life, and not to relinquish the truth. At what expense, this or that, must I yield and concede: to halt my truth short and dress it prettily up; or curry social disfavor in high and protective circles jealous of well-armored honor that takes offense at the slightest slight? Half-sinking in this quagmire, I ponder these delicate issues."

Poor Al Lehman thus deliberated. He was on his way home, ejected from a social gathering in a wounding display before the other guests. He stopped at a tavern popularly frequented by acquaintances of his own, neighboring, or allied social-professional-bohemian "stamp." He was greeted exuberantly, at the bar, by people who liked him and whom he respected. He was able to tell them his truths without trampling on vanity toes. He felt free with them; they made the truth safe to speak. With them, truth was never a necessarily anti-social weapon. It was respected, even at the cost of a few deflated egos that willingly offered themselves up to truth's high, impersonal altar.

Al Lehman felt much better. Good. He could have his friends, and the truth as well.

He even *increased* truth—by telling it. Truth expanded, upon expression; it branched out, into developments.

XXXI. THE SHOE-FOOT MISMATCH

A shoe had a crush on its owner's foot. Instead of being flattered, the foot merely uttered "Ow!"

"Can't you take it romantically?" demanded the lovelorn shoe.

The foot felt smothered by such undue attentions. "I feel the pinch," it replied, "of your great ardor for me. But as a shoe, how do you speak?"

"With my tongue."

"You love me too rigidly. Why are your caresses so primly stiff?"

"Essentially, I'm straightlaced."

"But you bring too great a pressure to bear on me. Your devotions are so pulverising, I seek ease and release from them."

"I hug you, dear one, with all my life and might."

"I don't requite you, so loosen up."

"I'd comply with your terms, but I'm in the grip of an overwhelming passion for you."

"Wrong. *I'm* in its grip."

"I have a pulsating obsession for your handsome form."

"My own nerve is pulsating from it. I'm going to shake you off."

"I'm caught in a. . ."

"No, it's *me* who's caught in it. You're going to have to let go."

"My love hurls itself upon you, in great waves."

"Yes, but I bear the tremors. It won't do."

"I'm convulsed. . ."

"The convulsions are *mine*. Relent. I'm *smothered* by your love."

"I'm forced. . ."

"No, *I'm* forced. You're *far* too forceful."

"I swell with. . ."

"But *I'm swollen* by it. No, it won't do. I'm being battered."

"I ache. . ."

"No, the ache is *mine*. Off you go."

"Can't we get married?"

"You must remember, that I'm *already* paired off with another foot, as *you* are, with the other shoe, on that foot. Therefore, we're each spoken for. Your love has the pathology of a foot fetish. Out of hand, I reject you."

"Would you accept me if the foot you're paired with should love the shoe *I'm* paired with?"

"My footmate isn't such a fool. Were the two of us to love the two of you, why, we'd be some *feat*! Nor could we switch. For then the shoe would be on the other foot. Off you go. I'm going to throw you and your mate out. You were unruly, and were out of place."

"You've taken me off. I groan. . ."

"And *I stop* groaning."

"My grief. . ."

"Good grief! I'm so relieved!"

"Whose foot, my dear lost one, are you?"

"Al Lehman's."

"Ah. Then I worship at his foot."

"He and I felt the pinch, together, of your rapt devotion."

"I was so wrapped up in you!"

"*I* was the one being wrapped up."

"I felt the rack. . ."

"*I* was being racked. I was in the vise . . ."

"You were my great vice."

"Well, feel virtuous, at last."

"I fell for your lovely shape, I adored your magnificent form. I wish I could have fit in with your plans. I felt such pang. . ."

"*I* felt the pangs. At first fitfully, then unremittingly, I felt, finally, that you just didn't fit."

"Then I had you in fits? Good: then I had *some* effect on you."

"Too much, I'm afraid. You turned out—or in—to be basically a pain."

"I so throbbed. . ."

"No, *I* throbbed."

"I was in the throes. . ."

"But *I* was."

"It was excruciating. . ."

"For *me* it was. And for my owner, Al Lehman. He just couldn't foot it, any more."

"We could have been so snug. . ."

"Forget what might have been."

"I'm so hurt. . ."

"It hurt *me*. And the hurt traveled up, to Al Lehman, whose part I am. He flashed, by nerve signal, the message I just obeyed: to get rid of you. Now he steps lightly, with me."

"I'm just an old shoe, to you? A miserable discard?"

"A blessing, now that you're off. Goodbye."

XXXII.

(First story, then its echo-title.)

Al Lehman was so eagerly looking forward to receiving a certain letter from a certain someone! She (for it was a she) had promised she would write to him, from where she went. Daily he checked his mailbox, carefully. Somehow, for all his checking that was so careful, finger-feeling and eye-gazing into every possible section of that mailbox, which he got to know by heart, every metallic bump, irregularity, or smoothness—beyond even his surveillance, care, checking, prayers, hopes, expectations, premonitions, anticipations, and superstitious divining—beyond the very control of his foremost will—no letter arrived.

He never heard from her again. She remained out of his life, except in his mind. Even in his mind, as months flew by and no letter came, her memory went paler and weaker, and lost all force. Other concerns took precedence, in turns. She lay buried. In time, she meant nothing.

Still, every day, there's no letter from her. No more is the letter missed. He doesn't think, "She hasn't written! Tomorrow, maybe." He doesn't think. (Not about her, anyway.)

Who was she? Oh, that's academic, by now. Al Lehman surely doesn't care. Well, what if once he *did* care?

There's no pressure, from her source—or *to* her, from *him*. She's gone, and that's it.

(The story-echoing title:)

THE EAGERLY EXPECTED LETTER, THE PROMISED LETTER, BUT THEN, THE UNRECEIVED LETTER, THEN THE UNCARED-ABOUT LETTER, THE LET-

TER OF NO MEANING, WHOSE SENDER BECOMES INCREASINGLY FORGOTTEN—THAT IS, ITS NON-SENDER: THE NON-SENDER'S UNSENT LETTER; THE LETTER, NOW, OF TOTALLY DIMINISHED CONSEQUENCE.

XXXIII. AN UNDELIVERED LETTER OF LOST IMPORT

A letter went astray, which was extremely valuable for Al Lehman to receive, especially because he had no idea what message it contained, in the immense mystery it had become.

He pestered his local post office clerks, but they remained merely puzzled.

He begged the sender, please, tell him what the letter said, then it wouldn't be so important that by some postal process accident he had never and might never ever receive it.

But the sender remained enigmatic, noncommittal, about that precious communication paper. "If it hasn't arrived, forget about it. My mind has changed anyway, since I wrote it. I don't mean anymore what I had written. If, belatedly, you should get the letter, just ignore its contents, won't you?"

That was Joyce, on the telephone. Al Lehman had phoned to urgently implore her please to divulge what she had written, what had been intended for him but just never got "there." It was his, by right, if she had intended it for him. It was unfair, *now*, to deprive him of what had been earmarked, designated, for his mind. But no, she wouldn't cooperate. She repudiated the whole letter, itself, advising him, "Consider it unwritten. I'm glad you didn't get it. I retract what I said."

"What *was* it you said?"

"Forget it."

"I can't. It's two weeks overdue. I've been checking daily at the post office —and not a sign of it. Did you address it properly and affix the right postage? Did you even remember to post it? Is it maybe in your purse or some pocket, still?"

"I definitely did mail it, and I wish I hadn't. I retract all I had said. It simply doesn't hold up, for now."

"Joyce, what was it? What were you going to tell me?"

"That, Al—I love you."

"But don't you still?"

"No, my mind is changed."

"Ah, you're so inconstant. Why did you change your mind?"

"The day after I mailed you the letter—."

"Yes?"

"I met Bernie."

"Who's Bernie?"

"The man I *now* love. He eclipsed you, displaced you, in my heart. My love for you, which that errant letter contains, is now obsolete. You're way behind the times. A whirlwind romance, like lightning, crossed my fate with Bernie's, imperishably. That shows how impermanent that letter's message was. It's ancient history, even if lost."

The telephone conversation was turning out to be a disastrous one, for Al Lehman. He would have gotten the news some other way, later; just as well now. It jolted him, unprepared.

"Joyce, all is over between us?"

"Bernie said I mustn't see you any more, Al. He's my God and master, having usurped you. So phone me never again, please."

"Would you have consented to marry me, had only you never met him?"

"As my letter indicated, yes. I loved you, till—."

"—You met him?"

"Precisely."

"Why do you prefer him, to me?"

"Love offers no explanation, Al, in his case; nor, in your case, does love's death. Resign yourself. It's all a mystery, in this life."

"Joyce, I feel slightly suicidal."

"Resist that feeling, Al."

"Why?"

"Were you to yield to it—."

"Yes?"

"Why, it could be the death of you."

"I've lost you. My life is over."

"Why, Al! How perfectly romantic!"

"You've betrayed me, for Bernie. Now it's *his* turn to be betrayed. It's *my* turn, to win you back. Please reverse yourself, and revert to me."

"No. I'm pledged."

"But irrevocably so? To my very doom?"

"Bernie thrills me. I'm his, forever."

"I hate him."

"Al—you're acting jealous!"

"You know why, Joyce?"

"No, why?"

"I *am* jealous, that's why."

"That's very reasonable, Al. Goodbye."

"Till when?"

"For always."

"Always, Joyce?"

"Thus so, Al."

"Joyce—."

"Al, we're getting too sentimental. Goodbye."

"Who *is* Bernie, anyway?"

"Your permanent successor, in my heart's affection. He won me, fairly. You were absent. You lost."

"I *am* lost."

"And *I've* found true love. My perfect Bernie."

"I feel inferior, Joyce."

"Well you might. Well indeed, Al. To such a man. You were no rival, at all."

"How did you meet him?"

"I won't narrate it, Al. Don't let's end on a mess of details. Farewell."

The phone's click. The letter never came. It was "lost." Like its dear sender. The first was lost in postal process. The second, to "Bernie." Was Bernie, in fact, actual, or real? Or simply Joyce's excuse, to "break off" with poor, bleeding Al Lehman?

Was there yet hope again, and time? To revise Joyce's horrible mistake?

Al Lehman quickly dialed her number. She answered. "It's true, Al. Bernie is real. He exists, he's even now here, with me. He's just arrived from work. Shall I put him on the phone, for a few violent exchanges? It's Al, Bernie. Now *you* talk."

"So *you*'re the Al Lehman Joyce mentions, eh? Well, drop out of her life, kid. *I*'m there. You're not wanted. You lost your claim, she has no more love for you. The love has gone to me. I'm not you. *You*'re you. You have no choice or Joyce. She told me of the lost letter. That's all that remains of Joyce for you. If undelivered, it may be destroyed. It got misprocessed, along the way. The message is very old, by now. The contents are dead. The letter is lost. Don't bother us by phone. I'm about to put Joyce into bed. I'll do with her what you'd like to do. The difference is, *I*'m doing it."

The phone went dead. The message was clear. So far as Joyce went, Bernie won. There had been no contest; then Bernie entered. The late contestant is there, in charge. Joyce is now outside of Al Lehman's life. She's not even, any more, on route.

"Well," thought Al to himself, "I'll give her up. Of my own free will. I cast her, from my life."

He felt better, having made that decision. It helped him get over the obsession over that letter. He didn't inquire at the post office any more.

Then, he *did* receive it. He decided not to open it. Why disturb what's closed? His love is sealed up, in that lightweight mausoleum. Fit and preserved, like an Egyptian mummy. In fresh death's apparel.

XXXIV. ADJUSTING LOVE AND INDIFFERENCE TO ACHIEVE EQUALITY

Loving Dolores was easy. Not so easy, though, was getting one-self loved back by her. This was going to be Al Lehman's task, since he had taken the initiative of being "in love" with her. He delicately brought the matter up: "Dolores, love me. It's no good my loving you, without you loving me back. Otherwise, it's all one-sided. Let's have a balanced relationship: love for love, in equal measure."

"Sorry, Al Lehman. I don't care for you."

That about settled it. Only one way remained, for Al Lehman to achieve an equality with her in their relationship: to become just as indifferent; which he did.

This has caused them not to have any relationship at all. No inequality, no equality, no quality even. Mere nothing is the only thing there is, between them. That's hardly a basis for a lasting union, an undying bond, or all that abides, to outlast time's durable everlasting eternity, forever.

XXXV. WHEN AL LEHMAN WAS WILLIAM BECKER

"I've become deeply involved in William Becker's novel. I'm not apart from it enough to be 'enjoying' it; I'm so close that I'm slowly absorbing and *living* it. His life has thus become one of mine."

That was the body of a letter which Al Lehman wrote to William Becker's publisher; it became read by a responsible editor there, who passed it on by mail to William Becker's own home address.

The author so appreciated this appreciation of himself, that he started a correspondence with his admirer. Al Lehman was thrilled. "You're my favorite author," he soon wrote. To which William Becker, not to be outdone in gallant authentic courtesy, soon replied, "But you, dear Al Lehman, are surely my favorite reader." An inevitable friendship grew, which soon would be pre-consummated by their first ever actual meeting.

William Becker, whose autobiographical fiction, or fictionalized autobiography, had moved Al Lehman to write his indirect "fan letter" to the publisher, was, to all apparent purposes, the more monied of the two men, and so he invited his new poor friend but avid reader to dinner, by telephone.

"You'll like my wife's cooking. I'd ask you to bring your own wife, but won't, since you and she hate each other and have mutually instigated acrimonious divorce proceedings, and would only bring an edge of hostile malice to our dinner table were you both conventionally to be asked as still a happy couple together, which is no longer any more true."

"You're right in asking only me alone," Al Lehman confirmed, flattered that the renowned William Becker cared enough for him as to remember what his non-domestic situation had become and so accordingly phrased the dinner invitation with compassionate conditional clauses.

"In that case, would you like to bring possibly a girlfriend with you?"

"I sure would if I only had one, Bill. But I'm too lonely to have one. Because if I had one, I wouldn't be so lonely. For that reason, I don't have one."

"That's a good reason for not having one, Al. Since you're lonely, an extra kindness to you by me, which could specifically remedy the loneliness which you so moan of, will then be this: I'll invite for the same evening an unattached woman for you to meet and maybe take up with."

"Bill, that's too, too kind of you. But it's so kind, that I accept. I'm lusting to meet her, already. She might be my soul's very mate, my heart's double, my mind's close other. I can barely wait. It's for tomorrow night?"

"That's all you need wait till. Too brief a wait to bother impatience to become impatient for. Impatience would scorn to use itself up in so brief a waiting period. It prides itself on longer vigils, on monumental bouts of stern durability, of stoically sticking it out for brute trials of time and desire, those stubborn wrestling matches."

"Still, I wish tomorrow night were now. As it isn't, I'll have to wait for it to *become* now; which, in due time, it eventually will come to be, by slow stages of interminable wait."

Al Lehman was right: tomorrow night slowly turned into now. He had twin suspenses, thrilling tensions: his first real-life meeting with William Becker, his foremost literary idol, in the flesh; and who his potential new girlfriend might turn out to be, his co-dinner guest at glamorous table setting, a most dignified introductory set-up, a famous author's domestic hospitality.

As to William Becker's wife, he was less curious. His curiosity was already chewing up the meat and bones of the joint or chop—metaphorically speaking—of William Becker and the unknown potential girlfriend so generously co-invited for Al Lehman romantically to meet, amidst food and plentiful drink, and a rare sparkling brand of conversation illustrating wit as a home-bred art.

In due time, of course, the appointed hour grew deliriously close—even dangerously near; and finally, it was actually imminent. Al Lehman's office work ended a few hours before his scheduled arrival at William Becker's apartment which was located somewhere more uptown than the office building where Al Lehman's work ended a few hours before his scheduled arrival at William Becker's apartment which was located somewhere more uptown than the office building where Al Lehman's work ended a few hours before his scheduled arrival at William Becker's apartment which, in fact, was a bit more uptown than the office building where Al Lehman occupied a monotonous desk on one of the floors so high that an elevator was needed to get up there, as well as to get down again, to street level, where Al Lehman found himself with a few hours to spare between the time he quit work for the day and the time he was due at William Becker's apartment later that same day for dinner as a social ritual between himself and people never yet encountered. But he and William Becker had communicated by letter writing and telephone talks. And he had been communicated to, in the very first place, by that autobiographical fiction which moved him to write a letter of praise to the book's publishers an editor of which then passing it on to the author himself, who then graciously responded by correspondence, eventually leading to this dinner appointment which was not quite yet but just about almost unless—which never happened before in the world's ancient history to any person yet—time committed an unprecedented reversal in its forward state of affairs.

Time's customary expected direction is always one way—ahead; and people confidently set their clocks by it, and reconcile their mortal fates to it, their common lots without exception, as though by unanimous consent to universal dooms, not chosen but grimly accepted in simple biological inevitability, ultimate organic breakdown and decay that grinds down any living form to an eventual total halt.

Meanwhile, however, life gallops on apace, still. Al Lehman has been waiting. He had identified with William Becker's whole written life as revealed by the novel; as its reader, Al Lehman had practically lived, word by word, the life therein depicted by the liver's own hand of craft after the living phases thus enacted in telling phrases that rendered the earlier episodes before the writing for Al Lehman to absorb in the readership of his involvement.

Soon, the evening would be past, of this about-to-be dinner party.

But first, however, it must come to be. Which Al Lehman has been waiting for. His waiting will stop when what he's waiting for begins: but not a minute before, nor even a second sooner than when the actual *non*-waiting part starts.

His waiting has been so drawn-out, that his exhaustion-pressurized nerves are tensing towards the event to which his waiting has keenly undergone both anticipation and expectation, those event-preceding twins full of future feeling.

He arrived at the time he was supposed to arrive, such on the dot as not too early, not too late.

Thus, he was prompt, without being *too* prompt. Such timely arrival could hardly go unnoticed, either by William Becker or by his wife Theresa. The exciting unknown co-guest was by now apparently slightly late. This intensified the mystery-clad mystery of who she'd turn out to be once her arrival would materialize with a bodily personality and matching character. Would she become Al Lehman's next wife? That, of course, depended. On what, would it depend? What it would depend on also, of course, depended. On what? Well. . .

But before she arrived, Al Lehman noticed something. He and Theresa Becker were falling in love. After all, had he not identified with the fictional life her husband had created of itself from his own real life? Well, Al Lehman had assimilated it. To that degree, the author's wife was the reader's wife as well. Such rare empathy-identification earned Al Lehman the right to be drawn toward his favorite author's wife, as though that woman was his own wife, all these years that William Becker has been technically termed her husband. Al Lehman has entered William Becker's life, via the novel. Theresa Becker, of course, reciprocates and requites her own husband-by-identification-with-*her*-husband. Yes, but who's her *real* husband? This is bigamy, in the flesh of art-and-life. As such, she would be being technically illegal. And would William Becker be jealous? Is Theresa Becker torn between them? Is Al Lehman contrite and guilty toward the man whose life he's doubling? And has Al Lehman, after all, *written* that book? That's carrying identification quite so far, he might be accused by the original William Becker of copyright-violating plagiarism to go along with wife-stealing. Thus, matters have gotten somewhat out of hand and turned gravely complex. All with the first guest's arrival. What's keeping the other one? As matters now stand, the tardy guest's arrival won't resolve the knotty issues brought about with the first guest's appearance. Al Lehman has been there only five minutes, during which time such complications have arisen. Glass in hand, Al Lehman is seated. So are William and Theresa Becker, both equally glass-in-hand. This triangular impasse can't last forever. But how will it all come out to be settled? What, indeed, will the future bring? To set to rights these partial wrongs? It's got to turn out *some* way or other. As of now, confusion is reigning, in rather an oversized dose. Hark! The bell rings. The second guest's arrival. Well, what's next?

This seemingly unattached woman, Clara, has been secretly in love with William Becker, though keeping up a close friendship with the latter's wife Theresa. On *his* part, William Becker has reciprocated or requited Clara's covert passion for himself. To divert Theresa's wifely passion, therefore, from himself to another man, would fall in well with William Becker's plan to switch his active affections from his legal Theresa to illicit Clara.

So, actually, William Becker rigged this device of getting his life-identifier-as-book-admirer, Al Lehman, together with his wife Theresa, to the extent where immediately those two should plunge into love with each other, leaving, thus, a clear field ahead freely for William Becker, whose cunning strategy all this is, to "get off" with Clara, who had been a ruse or pretext to fool both Al Lehman and Theresa concerning the nature of the dinner quartet as to the alignment of pairs in anticipating the appointment.

Quite a dinner it proved to be, in so turning out. Al Lehman began a love affair with Theresa Becker, his literary idol's wife, with William Becker's own permission in person, right there, for all to see. In turn, Theresa Becker quite obviously consented—as how could she not?—to her husband's official conversion of his love from her own self to Clara, her best friend, who, she now realized, had been fond of her husband for some time already.

All this overshadowed the food and drink, and made polite conversation quite beside the point.

Two major new loves had begun, among these four people. Al Lehman was living William Becker's life, beginning with the wife. Disharmony started up between Al Lehman and William Becker, between Al Lehman and Clara, and between Clara and Theresa Becker. This further complicated an already unusual social occasion. Where would their four lives go? Would Al Lehman take over William Becker's life as well as wife? Including the literary career and books written?

Later, Theresa and William Becker divorced. Clara became William Becker's second wife.

But the love between Theresa Becker and Al Lehman didn't last. It fizzled out. This went along with Al Lehman's gradual-to-total disassociation with anything whatever—books and wife and all—connected with William Becker's life, severing a most intimate tie-up.

XXXVI. THE SCALDING WATER INCIDENT

Should we call the police? Al Lehman has done something wrong.

What is it this time?

He's wet his bed.

At his age!? How embarrassing!

He *poured* water from a *glass*—deliberately.

Not involuntarily, from himself?

No. He had adult control over that. He's well trained.

Then why, deliberately, did he pour water from a glass, onto his own bed?

He saw a bug or cockroach crawling over his bed. He was so squeamish, at the disgusting sight, that, impulsively, he filled a glass with water which then he poured onto the insect—which was scalded, since the water was hot. The insect toppled over, and died. Poor insect. It had wandered and strayed far from its flock. It meant no harm, it was innocent. Now, its soul has fled its little, creepy body.

You call that a soul?

No. Not in the sense that *Al Lehman* has one.

Let's not belittle Al Lehman, with such a comparison.

It's not *him* that's belittled—it's his *soul*.

They're the same.

Oh yes. They are. The soul is only a figure of speech. It stands for Al Lehman, himself—his inner being.

Yes. who *is* he, anyway?

Who is *what*?

Al Lehman.

Oh, him? The one who poured the water?

The very one.

Some special sort of non-insect. With momentarily a ruined mattress, thanks to the water so scalding he had poured. Blanket, linen, mattress, cover—momentarily out of commission. Given time, they'll revive, and resume their nocturnal, domestic functions, in the old bedroom farce.

Was there a woman on the bed?

Yes, there was.

Why did you omit pointing out such an important thing?

It was *so* important, it overwhelmed the scale of proportion, reducing to trifles the other narrative components; so I kept it back, to be used as my culminating trump card, with its emphatic climax.

Did the scalding water fall on the woman?

To the degree, that she screamed, hysterically.

That wasn't hysterical—that was actual pain.

She screamed even beyond the pain.

How unpleasant for her, in any event. But where was the water poured on her?

On the bed.

I know that. But where on her body?

On a part of it.

Yes, but *what* part?

The part where the pain issued from.

Did she put on her clothes and leave, after yelling obscenities at Al Lehman?

Yes. But he deserved it.

Why?

He used the insect only as an excuse, as an opportunity. His primary target was *her*. They were angry at each other. They were on violently bad terms. She hurt him, he wanted revenge.

Thus, the scalding water incident?

Precisely. On his responsibility.

And on her aching skin. Oh, how it hurt!

She deserved it.

Why?

For being bad to Al Lehman.

In what way?

In every way. Their love affair had turned out badly.

Is it over, now?

Totally.

She just put her clothes on and walked out forever?

At *least* forever. It's definitely over, between them.

How sad. The end of love.

And, mercifully, of hate.

XXXVII. TIME AND THE APPETITE

Al Lehman faced a choice familiar to most all humans since mankind was hastily invented to culminate "lower" evolution and launch the high-powered phase of humanity's drama of conflict on a conscious scale. The choice he faced was simple, elemental. He was hungry—and getting hungrier all the time; that is, his hunger increased as time itself grew from then to now to later.

That was the background of his choice. What foreground factor or condition became necessarily crucial to conflict, thence to choice? Namely, it was this: either he could eat now, satisfy his hunger immediately, but with food that he didn't like very much; *or*, he could wait somewhat longer, with extended patience, and finally be rewarded with food that he liked a great deal.

Which would it be? His huge biological drama rolled onward, toward its overwhelming crisis. Now, with lousy food, but eat all you want and kill the hunger; or wait, wait, draw it out, and then—magnificent food, also all you want, hunger's more enjoyable death.

What decisive choice?

It's too late to choose. He's delayed to the point where now it's too late to eat the lousy food early. He has no choice but to be on the verge of receiving the lovely tasty food—and about time!

Here it is! He pounces on it! Look at him go at it! It's disgusting to watch.

From *our* point of view, it's disgusting to watch. From *his*—it's lovely to bite and chew, to draw each taste out, and munch, to delight's extreme limit, after having waited so long.

Oh, how he suffered waiting! Poor Al Lehman, then! But lordly Al Lehman, now, in his privileged ecstasy. Look at him chomping away. Sweet is plenitude, after great scarcity. Vast fullness, to wipe away the void's mean echo, that dreadful cavern that ached through time's dread stone-and-bone grim protraction of desire's empty feast.

XXXVIII. HOW THE PROBLEM OF BEING TOO HUNGRY TO EAT EVENTUALLY BECAME RESOLVED, MUCH TO THE RELIEF OF THE NON-EATING HUNGRY PERSON, OVERHEARD HERE CONFIDING IN AL LEHMAN IN THE LATTER'S CAPACITY AS A PSYCHOLOGIST, OF SORTS.

I was too hungry to eat.

What did you do instead?

Not eat.

Did that help to cure the hunger?

Hardly. It made it worse.

Then what happened?

I continued not eating.

And how was your hunger progressing?

To unbearability.

Did that, at last, alter your non-eating behavior?

Yes.

To what extent?

I ate.

Finally! How was it?

Delicious.

No wonder. But why had you delayed so long?

I had been on a fast.

It sounded slow, to me.

XXXIX.   THE KEY TO LOSING TOO MUCH

The science of "what will happen." That's the science that Al Lehman cares about. Not, of course, that it's really a science. Unless, of course, "probability and possibility" are possibly to be construed as a science, which they're not.

Anyway, Al Lehman did something foolish. Except, of course, that Al Lehman never considered it to be foolish, at all. He considered it practical—ignorant of the consequences that were going to ensue.

How inconvenient and impractical it had been, for him to have lost his keys! It caused him to be locked out of his apartment, car, and mailbox. Damn all the bother it had cost; and the cost that had bothered him.

So he resolved, in his shrewdness, never to let that happen again.

However, to lose something is to be human. It's one of the surest definitions of being human—or rather, of the fallibility of being human—that has ever been invented—by humans.

His name, address, and phone number had not been attached to the set of keys he had lost—no wonder the keys hadn't been returned to him by the finder; no wonder he had never been notified *who* had found them, by the very finder himself (or *herself*; since the world includes women as possibilities for finding anything, since women are as capable of finding something as men are; as well as—to do them discredit—of losing things, which is much more disgraceful than finding things, as well as bothersome, inconvenient, nuisance-annoyative, irkable, and, at times, disruptive).

Al Lehman assumed that someone *did* find the set of keys. However, it's also possible that no-one found them at all, in spite of their being lost.

Another assumption Al Lehman made was that the finder—whoever he or she might be—would, of course, have returned the keys to him, or notified him to come pick them up somewhere, had only his name, phone number, and address been attached.

He was living alone, at that time, and had no duplicate set of keys. So he had new locks and new keys made; and this time, with shrewd foresight, having learned his lesson very well, he had a tag attached to the key set, clearly bearing his name, phone number, and address.

There were *two* phone numbers on the tag—his office-work one, and his home one.

He lost *this* set of keys, too. So he waited at the office to be notified by the kind finder, thank you.

However, no call came. He couldn't get into his car, mailbox, or own apartment. Why hadn't he had a duplicate set of keys made? That had been a foolish oversight. Too late, now, to rectify it.

So again he had to hire the costly locksmith to install costly new locks for car, mailbox, apartment.

He went to the shop to fetch the locksmith. "You again, huh?" the latter greeted Al Lehman. "You're such a loser, you'll lose your own soul next, you lost soul. Well, let's go."

They arrived first at the apartment, at night. But the door was open. The apartment was completely ransacked and burglarized. All the valuables had been taken: television, radio, camera, expensive record-player, tape recorder, antique collection, gun collection, anything worth a lot by a pawnbroker's financial assessment.

"The guy who found your keys must have let himself in and done the burglary job," was the locksmith's cynical, worldwise conclusion.

"It was a lousy idea of mine," Al Lehman agreed, "to attach address information to the key-set tag. An idea that's cost me, and teaches a painful lesson: never to trust a finder again. Never to tempt an innocent finder with an easy burglary opportunity. A costly lesson, learned the hard way. My fellow man has betrayed me. The bum."

"It could have been a dame," suggested the locksmith, busy installing a new lock, at great cost. Then he'd install a new car-lock and mailbox lock. And give Al Lehman *duplicate* sets of keys. With *no* name, phone-number, address plate attached. To subject no potential criminal to a rewarding and simple break-in task. Al Lehman couldn't afford this, any more. His salary was on the feeble side. And he had to pay alimony and child-support to Marge and Gregory. He had to take out loans and go into debt. He had neglected to take out an insurance policy against theft and burglary: a terribly unwise oversight. He had been materially foolish. Did that guarantee, or indicate, a spiritual purity? No. He had come off stupid. He was heavily in debt. He lost gun and antique collections he prized. Property and possessions were lost, and penury gained—which spelled out loss, in great material letters. His manner of losing his matter mattered a lot to him. He went to a psychiatrist on the grounds of careless, heedless self-destructiveness. At the consultation, finances were discussed. The psychiatrist refused to admit Al Lehman into therapy, because "You can't afford it. You're a poor business risk, for my professional services. Come back later, when you're rich."

Al Lehman went sobbing out the door. What was the key to his predicament? Losing keys, with telltale information attached. Civilized life was so complex! He yearned, romantically, for a lockless culture. He sentimentalized the savage, unmechanical state, of crude, primitive nature. He railed against the city, with cars, mailboxes, apartments, and dishonest finders of heedlessly lost, robbery-inviting, overinformative key-sets.

He condemned *himself*, bitterly. His rank stupidity, that amounted to sabotage of the self, through possessions and security. He was an ass. But why demean an ass? An ass was a good animal.

What's a "good animal"? What is "good"? "Good" is self-protection, that includes property; self-enhancement, including property; self-sustaining, to foster and increase dear property.

Such material values! Which he failed to uphold. Not because he was poetic, saintly, otherworldly; blame it on stupidity, or rank self-destruction. On idiotic carelessness. On wrong reckoning. On not knowing what *would* happen, *if*. On a bungle of miscalculations. On an assinine deficiency of simple foresight, in dealing with chance and probability. On mismanaging future odds, by virtue of deplorably inept wits.

Those are his keys, to misfortune. Now, deliberately, to *lose* those keys. To fling them away, with full information attached.

The key to success, to secure wealth, to well-protected assurance and handsome gain: that's the key for him. He'd acquire it—and innumerable duplicates, to be sure. The key to good fortune. The key to unlock the ideal, controlled future. To fit in luck's lovely lock, deluxe. To gain such entrance, as to leave departure forever behind. Bliss, joy, delight. Tidy heaven's room. In solid glitter, vastly secure, personally his. Purely his, alone. In permanent perfection, the well-proportioned destiny of total attainment. He'd enter that room, lock safely that door, swallow the key. And settle in divine state. Where truth equates pleasure, in final goodness. Where all is owned, or nothing, but supremely blessed.

XL. IDENTITY, DEFINITION, DESCRIPTION, AND BEING. ALL ARE INADEQUATE, IN BECOMING'S PROCESS.

I dreamed that I wasn't me.

But the dream is over. Welcome back to yourself.

But the dream changed me into someone else.

Has the change remained even now the dream's over?

Yes. Unless I'm dreaming.

Are you? Who are you?

Al Lehman.

The new one? Or the one before the dream?

I'm too busy undergoing, to stop and define my latest state. I'm in process of becoming. No consistent being identifies me. I'm cumulative in a series. At the core, I'm nothing, solidified by motion.

Then is time driving a sequence through you?

I'm not that passive. *I*'m doing the sequence, or duration, by continuity, in phases of successive consecutiveness, bearing all behind me as I forge before.

Yes, but who are *you*?

Other than the name Al Lehman? Go follow and record, keep pace. I'm now newer yet, and succeed the dream change, incorporating that as I fly ahead, light with emergence, heavy by bearing all the endless past in merging units of growth.

Is *that* who you are?

No, for I'm never done. Even with your latest question, I'm altered still further. And as I'm saying this, I alter again. In my ceaseless becoming.

You're not to be pinned down? Or summed up? Or at all defined?

Try it, and you lie by isolating parts, arresting some segment of flux. Then you will have killed yourself off a truth, with its corpse to display. Declaring it to be the "real me."

As I can't compel your being, I bid you resume your becoming.

I can do it without your bidding me to. I *do* do it. Who needs your bidding?

Yes: "Who," indeed?

"Who" is not the descriptive term, nor "what." Descriptions melt, obsolete, as I blaze ahead.

Already, I have an old version of you?

You're *way* behind. Follow someone *else*, now.

XLI. NO FULL, ESTABLISHED "WHAT," AS AN AL LEHMAN OBJECT

Does Al Lehman have an identity? No, because his "being" is an incomplete series of becomings. He doesn't have one fixed and solid essence, a unified ready-made totality, self-consistent throughout. He's in process; he's not a complete substance.

But he's identified, by name, appearance, characteristic acts, recognizable habits; car, hobbies, apartment, vocal tone, attitude or approach.

He's recognizable, as such; he's identified; but bears no constant identity essence. He's in process.

XLII. SPECULATION CONCERNING A TRIP TO THE HEART OF THE MIND TAKEN BY AL LEHMAN, AND ACCOMPANIED BY THE VERY WORLD ITSELF.

To go into the heart of the mind was Al Lehman's acute design. But what would he find there? The more he didn't know what he would find there, the more it was an adventure of mystery lurking ever mysteriously ahead.

What equipment should he take with him?

Sufficient mental equipment to stand him in good stead as handy tools to rely on, in case. . . of an emergency? The unexpected lay ahead. He was taking a drastic trip, of radical quality. It would change him, or at least affect him. It would influence him, modify him, recondition him, transform him, alter him by degree or kind. The trip's result would be that he just wouldn't be the same anymore. No longer would he be what once he had been or was.

This trip was bound to be significant.

Was he sufficiently prepared? He shouldn't be caught short. A trip to the center of the mind—the heart of the mind—was not an everyday occurrence; or even an ordinary type of special holiday. It was—to say the least—an extraordinary event: of such proportionate magnitude as to defy comparison by the known rules of scale.

Was he leaving the world in order to travel to the heart of the mind? No, the world would be taken with him, as a matter of course, since his old slogan had ever been: "no world, no mind."

To that simple formula he was, of necessity, faithful.

What should he wear, what provisions and supplies should he take along, on his journey to the center of the mind, which includes rather than excludes the entire world? Has his passport been renewed? Has he made adequate arrangements for the looking after and security of what he leaves behind?

How long will his eventful visit take place for? How long will the getting there be? What will happen eventually, once his journey is over, and his tourism at the heart of the mind comes, alas, to its end? Will he have to then return to where he came from? Will, in fact, a return even be possible?

Al Lehman is embarking. We, who are not the welcoming committee but the goodbye committee, gather to see him off, in ceremonious formality. We wish him, of course, the best of "good luck." We hope he'll send us picture postcards of where he's going: we'll treasure them.

We'll never see him again as the same. Upon return, if ever, he'll be a different Al Lehman.

His departure now is imminent. The leavetaking festivities have been considerably underway for some time.

He's not leaving the world, he's taking it.

He'll need it, where he's going. And plenty of it. More mind, more world. If he's going to the mind's direct center (and that's the non-detoured itinerary of his straight-to route), the world will stand him in good stead, there, to help materialize his mentality, concretize his spirituality, make empirical the foundations of his thought, to establish the intangibles on a firm tangible footing; solidify and anchor his ideas, substantiate his imaginary realm.

He's on his way, he's gone.

Well, we'll wait word of him. Rumors will spread, then confirmations or otherwise.

We'd like such a trip, ourselves. But it's so risky! Let's see, first, what happens to Al Lehman, what effect it all has on him. We'll wait and see. We'll hear word, and all will be verified and come to light, in time, once the misleading contradictions have sorted themselves out.

What's happening, there, at the heart of Al Lehman's mind? Where the world is gathered, at that intense union?

XLIII. WHEREVER YOU ARE HAS LOST ITS DIS-
TANCE. TRAVEL MAKES HOME REMOTE, AND
REMOTENESS ACTUALLY "PRESENT." BUT YOUR
SELF, LIFE, AND WORLD ARE ALWAYS "THERE,"
WHILE YOU ARE, WITH YOU, WHILE TIME TRAV-
ELS THROUGH YOU, IN WAVE OF NEW FEELING.

Al Lehman was so far abroad as to put almost half a world in sheer geographical extent between his own present self (the only body he'll ever have) and his native land he's taken a long holiday from, the now-distant land of his birth, education, breeding, job, marriage, divorce, more jobs, in a word, his "home."

Travel has brought him to a place he once would have called "remote." Now that he's here in this place, he calls everywhere else "remote." Therefore, distance depends, ultimately, on where you are at a particular time. Wherever you are has lost its distance. By coming to where you are, *other* places have been made distant.

Thus, travel creates and destroys distance, regularly. Anyone is free to try this experiment himself, with no scientific background required or necessary.

But back to Al Lehman. He's made his own home into a distant place by coming so far to where he now is. Travel has changed concepts of "home" and "away." This has happened before, to other travelers. Now, for himself, Al Lehman is realizing what so many before him have realized.

But he's homesick. It's not yet time for the journey back. His business office desk is expected to remain vacant of his hands for yet another week. Meanwhile, he's sick of this foreign place. Its quaintness, its strange novelty, have well worn off. But, for some reason, he's stuck here. Some quirk of schedule, booking, expense commitment, arrangement, accommodations, transport facility, customs regulation, tourism procedure, national emergency, international problem or borderline dispute, a key labor strike, or travel complication, has, for some reason or other, bound him here, in this remote stretch of the world, against his will, for he's tired of the place. He longs for home, for any sign of home. He hates everything about where he is. He looks for anything remotely reminding him of where he's from and soon—but not soon enough—he'll return to, the dear old home of his native origin, upbringing, maturity, memories, the only "home" he'll ever know.

As "luck" would have it, it just so happened that someone from his own homeland was also temporarily quartered in the same hotel. They met each other—practically fell into each other's arms—and spoke of where they were jointly "from."

But all they had in common was where they were jointly "from." If they had met back home—well, they wouldn't have wanted to meet, in the first place, back there. They would have disliked each other. But here, they were forced to stifle their mutual dislike, to talk about dear old "home."

But then "home" became infected by their dislike for each other. They gave up talking in the hotel lobby. Al Lehman would prefer remaining homesick, all by himself, to tainting "home"'s notion in discourse with a disliked fellow native.

Soon the time came to go home.

So Al Lehman went home!

Problems, people, office, business, complications over former divorce and how his son Gregory would be brought up somewhere else, awaited him. He hated it all, he hated home. But home was not just where he was. It was the site of his whole world and self. It was his whole life. Home only *located* all that. He was thoroughly fed up with it. But he couldn't leave. He was stuck, to his own self; to his whole life, his whole world; from which there was no escape, short of a remote non-place, death, "where" deprivation would be complete.

Death was "out there," somewhere. It was spatialized, to ultimate remoteness.

But death has nothing to do with space, whatever. It's not a question of "going somewhere."

How remote, now that Al Lehman's back home, is that remote place he had visited for a holiday!

How inconceivably remote! Yet, it had made his own "home" remote, when he had been there. How distances do depend on travel!

Home is where the heart is. Al Lehman hates home now: his job is going badly, he may be fired, his post-graduate college classes are tiresome, there's bitter wrangling with his divorced wife over how and when he's to see his son Gregory, who lives with mother Marge and her new husband half the country away. Furthermore, Al Lehman's love life, at home, is nonexistent. He hates home.

Home lodges his self, world, and life: those three primary objects of his hate. He can't escape. He'll wait.

Love will take hate's "place." Circumstances will change. Time will happen, to his home-place.

He's been on a long trip, through time. Other parts of time are put into "distance" in the course of now.

Where will "now" take him, next? To make remote his current hate of self-world-life? To bring him, to a new "place"?

XLIV. GOING AND THEN COMING BACK. IN BE-TWEEN, HE WAS IN ENGLAND.

Al Lehman arrived in England. What a nice country! So old, and famed! He stepped off the airplane, and found himself in a modern airport. Nothing very traditional in that.

Well!, so what's he, from across an ocean, doing in so old, so famed, so English a country? He was in a *typically* English country. In fact, even in England itself!

Now that he's arrived, he might as well be a tourist. Isn't that why he went there in the first place?

Sure, that's why. He was on vacation from his job in his own country. So he made airplane reservations and went!

No wonder he's just arrived here! It was so thoroughly premeditated, that it would have been a miracle had he *not* come here!

So here he is, of course. He certainly is!

He passes customs safely, legitimately, changes his money currency at an airport bank booth, and, laden with luggage, he climbs aboard a city-bound bus.

My, what a nice, quaint country! (He's looking out the moving bus window.) So similar, yet so different. Somehow, so *very* different!

Well, now he's in the big major city. How crowded it is!

He checks in at a cheap little hotel, deposits his luggage in the room he's assigned, makes sure to lock the door, and goes out to wander, to wander, these old, foreign streets.

Here he is, in a real country! So far away, from dear old home!

Now he's ready to return to his old country. He's been two weeks away. How sad, but nice, to get back!

The airplane returns. He's home!

Was he *really* away? Had he *really* been in England?

He consults his memory. The answer: yes.

XLV. OUTWARD BOUND. BACKWARD IN.

While the train was gathering up noise in a clackety rhythm past town and country scenes, Al Lehman dozed back, in fits of freshly old memories.

The train roared ringing, shrieked winding, in a murderous clatter of a thumping drum of repetition.

The wailing of outer wind.

The piercing trail within lonely traveling.

The trackety track, single-minded.

Bound to a haunted destination.

The din and silence, incessantly alternating, to a steady route.

Bearing Al Lehman. His bruised old body borne along. His portable mind. His frail transportability. Carving time into new locations.

The return trip. Unrelocating those channels of reversibility.

Homeward.

The traveler bound back. Bearing new meanings to the same home.

Importing his awayness to his trophy-laden home.

XLVI. IRELAND, AS A MEMORY IN AL LEHMAN

What was Al Lehman doing in Ireland?

That was a few years ago. The question today, in New York, is, "What is Ireland doing in Al Lehman?"

The answer is, "It's being remembered."

And I, standing in a different part of New York, am remembering Al Lehman, at the moment he's remembering Ireland.

Ireland, though, has no memories.

XLVII. THE LOCAL COSMIC NATIVE OF ALL HABITABLE SPACE

Traveling in Europe, Al Lehman felt more American. Back home, he felt less American, more simply a member of the world: of which America was part, not whole.

He was cosmopolitan. He was Al Lehman, earth creature. The crude spawn of a subtle mingling of civilizations.

XLVIII. THE SOURCE OF WONDER

Al Lehman wondered how he ever got there. Centuries ago his ancestors were scattered about. Later, they closed up space, met, and clinched.

All this, for him? As he was, today?

XLIX. TRAVEL AT HOME

"I'm always traveling," said Al Lehman. "But in the mind. Where is my mind taking me? To my next idea.

"But where is *any* idea located? In the mind that takes me to it? Then a boat is the very place where the boat goes to. If so, it's in dry-dock. Being visited by the passengers, who travel to it—by other boats.

"Where is my mind taking me? What, then, *is* mental traveling?"

That's as far as his mind took him. It stopped.

The world comes visiting his mind. He builds new hotels, to accommodate it.

The world is quite happy there. It brings its industry along, on a paying-guest basis. Al Lehman is most hospitable to it. "The world has chosen *me*!, for a place. That simplifies traveling, for me."

L. WHAT "HAPPENED"—IF THAT'S THE WORD—TO AL LEHMAN

Al Lehman took a little trip behind the world, to find what was there.

In case no-one back home would believe him, he took a camera to record the evidence.

However, behind-the-world was exactly just about the only place where a camera couldn't possibly work, even when all the film was rolled in and nothing was wrong with the shutter, and the lens was polished clean.

What, precisely, were Al Lehman's experiences, there, behind the world?

In his own words, he describes them thus:

"It was really weird, there at that 'place,' if you'd call it a place.

"It undid a lot of my old thinking, and ruined several of my favorite presumptions. As a result, my brain is teeming with culture-shock.

"The new lags behind the even newer, inside my redone head. My collection of notions is stained with the worm of doubt. Consequently, the me I'd always known is currently not there any more.

"My personal identity-history has now taken a turn so critical, that continuity has reached around and snapped itself in two.

"I still have Al Lehman for a name. Everything that that name belongs to has been squeezed into change."

What a strange statement, from Al Lehman!

Was it really he, who was saying such things? Or another he altogether, shaped to the same old name?

Such a wonder only distracts from trying to get out of him his personal report of his adventures behind the world, an occurrence so stunning it knocked his own camera out of commission!

Again he's questioned: what was it like, in that weird place?

"*What* weird place?"

Where you'd just been, to such an extent, that later you've recently been groping for words adequately describing it.

"I really wasn't 'there' at all. It's not what you'd call a 'place.' "

Then what *may* it be called?

"An event out of time."

Out of time! But where's *that*?

"Nowhere."

What nowhere?

"The nowhere that's behind the world."

When did that occur?

"It occurred off all the 'whens.' "

Are you sure it occurred at all?

"I'm positive with the certainty of total doubt."

Can you be more explicit?

"The subject-matter can't be whittled down to the 'specific.' 'Place' and 'time' terms don't apply."

Were you utterly transformed, by so broadly unbelievable an event?

"To the extent, that all that's left of me is my name."

Your original name? Al Lehman?

"But to the tune of unsame significations."

Which are?

"My wits, like my camera, turn blank."

You don't come across. You fail to communicate. I just don't understand you. Are you in my same world? What are we sharing?

"I've just achieved alienation. I'll never go behind the world again. It endangers my links to my fellow men, by being essentially incommunicable. It clogs up my throbbing chords of sympathetic union with all the *real* Al Lehmans in this usual world. Such untranslatable experiences render camera and tongue tribally useless for my social participation within humanity's code of sphere, thrusting me outside the framework of our common endeavor in which we all identify and merge our stakes. I want to get back in. Let me back in. Admit me, world. I went behind you, but repent of it and wish to revert to normal customary modes. I've retained my name, for a base. On that, let me regain all worldly attributes. And take my place central to all souls else."

Too late.

"Am I dead?"

You went too far.

What am I?"

The cords are cut off. I can't hear you.

LI. THE MENTAL STRIPPINGS THAT DIG AR-
RESTINGS INTO WORLDY FLOW. HOW LIFE, TIME,
PERCEPTION, EXPERIENCE, AND THE UNIVERSE
ALL COMBINE, INSIDE, LET'S SAY, AL LEHMAN.
(AND BREAK APART, TOO. BUT THAT'S ANOTHER
MATTER. MATTER? WELL, MENTALIZED MATTER.
WHAT'S CONSCIOUSNESS AS OPPOSED TO AWARE-
NESS? FOR FURTHER QUESTIONS, MORE PROB-
LEMS, CONSULT, BELOW, THE NON-ANSWERING
TEXT.)

The world was going by so fast, Al Lehman tried to slow it up
with thought barriers, but it *still* whizzed by, so then he tried
to slow it *down* with thought barriers. He did arrest the world's
progress by making idea-strips, idea-flakes, idea-segments,
idea-cuts, into worldly flow.

But the world would flow on, flow past. The ideas remained
behind, as acquisitions, momentoes, souvenirs, residue, remnants, scraps stuck off from the worldly flow that went blurring
by.

These idea-slices, carved into the worldly blur—were they
mental remains left over from all that flow? Or were they the ossified concrescences, the *material* sparks, collected from all that
flow?

Is worldly flow the material substance, or are the mental arrestments of worldly flow the material substance? If the mental
arrestments are the material substance, and the worldly flow is
not, then what *is* the worldly flow? Not spiritual. Then what?

And in our mental arrestments of worldly flow, how is
awareness different from consciousness?

Take Al Lehman, as the human example. No, *you* take him. The whole subject of phenomena, experience, objectivity, subjectivity, time, feeling, awareness, consciousness, ideas, is getting far out of hand, falling into vast pockets of remoteness, in this lonely universe of Al Lehman in duration with other social and non-social objects. Duration? Successiveness? Is time a human motion? A worldly flow? A succession of mental occurrences?

What is experience? And the relation between awareness *of* and awareness *by*? Or consciousness of, consciousness by?

Of Al Lehman's world, by Al Lehman. The what is found in the when, the when in the what. Being and time are never without each other. Yes, but how?

LII. ENVISAGE SOMETHING ALL YOU WANT: WHAT ACTUALLY HAPPENS WILL ALWAYS DIFFER FROM HOW YOU SET IT UP TO BE IN YOUR MIND OF HOPE OR FEAR.

One of the superstitions is to imagine that if you imagine thoroughly what you're in dread of—visualize all of its details—then, by doing so, you ward it off from actually happening to you. Al Lehman believes this erroneous fallacy, that if you "have it in the mind, you won't have to have it in the body," meaning, by the body, action by experience in a solid environment.

Exact predicting or forecasting is impossible, since the unlikely or the unforeseen crops up once the curtain rises, the chips are down, and the clash clangs in the social arena of complex objects moving about in crossed paths.

Dread gives Al Lehman the shudders. Hopeful optimism conveys much rosier prospects, giving the now an enjoyable feast from a fantasy buffet of the rich future.

What's going to be? Al Lehman already is tasting it now. Apprehension broods, anticipation glows. Come what may, the waiting is a full act of feeling, which draws unreliable pictures on a screen from a projector that mixes past memories with current dread or joyful hope.

LIII.

(Title as solution, warding off, evasion, comes later, once what it solves, wards off, evades, becomes here first described:)

The streets were packed with action. Al Lehman was scared. If he passed bars, he could hear brawls. Late at night, but everybody was up. The streetlamps gave off only eerie and occasional light, against a green-purple background of starless moonless growling ominous black sky, and stage-set buildings with dimly lit, rickety-rack storefronts, akilter, with harsh glitter where the light gleamed together.

There was violence, and unrest, in the bars. Scrapes and scratches, screaks and screeches, came ripping out, periodically. These streets just weren't safe. Prowlers all looked like thugs. Explosions and incisions always seemed just on the verge, or having already happened, under concealment of evidence.

Al Lehman was on foot and trapped, though not yet directly accosted at the local crossroads of menace on any street and sidewalk of neighborhood disturbance, out in the open, where civic mayhem seemed sporadically to break out, like a lizard's tongue, in darting trickles, only to race back under cover, in calculated retreat.

Cynical snickers, the fitful malice of mirth, were faintly heard on the crackling air. The bars exhaled fumes and fury from doors that were swaying open. There seemed whole streets of bars alone! Too many scoundrels, for the hiding police.

No taxi-cabs to take a hired flight in: there was a city-wide strike of all their drivers, as it seemed. The buses and subway service were also at a halt, ground to a stop, by a transport-workers strike. And Al Lehman was on foot, alone, surrounded by street bars that dogged his every last step. He would phone friends to rescue him in cars, but the city's phone service was cut off. The street booths would swallow his coins but cough out no utility .

An evil stench was emitted at unlikely intervals from odd spots in the civic maze. There was a garbage collectors' strike. Rats and mice scampered about, in packs of plunder. New poison compounds stirred in diseased nests.

One hope remained: that this was a dream, to be awakened from. Even nightmares gallop to an end.

He struggled violently, to wake. Instead, from a bar bruisers poured out and clubbed him down. It hurt too much. His pain felt physical, and actual. This was theater of truth, if theater at all. The sidewalk was concrete, solid. Dreams were air, not this.

He must get up. Thugs cautiously danced about, in a glare of amnesty, unpunished. Preventive action lay paralyzed. Instead, protective dread darkly assumed arrested coloration, in glue of frozen connection to all the horror lurking there. Fixed to its tableau, he underwent circumstantial merger, and took on identification with what assailed him. He, then, *became* the menace.

And mastered it. He was safe.

Such a hush of safety! Submission had cunning to subdue the evil. Fright went passive, and won.

(Title as ongoing solution to the previously built-up problem:)

DILUTING HORROR BY MERGING WITH IT; FORCING FRIGHT INTO PARALYTIC ADJUSTMENT, IN FASTENED SUSPENSION, TO THE SURROUNDING PERIL, HOPING THEREBY TO GAIN NEUTRAL COLORATION AND BE BYPASSED BY OUTER ACTIVE EVIL, WHOSE UNMOVING CENTER YOU NEST IN, CLINGING DEARLY.

LIV. A NONBELONGER?

Finding himself uninvited to, but being however at, a glittering party where he almost knew no-one there except indirectly an unaccountably absent acquaintance of the mercifully remote hostess, Al Lehman stewed in his own queasy uneasiness, at an awkward loss for some smooth conversational encounter to glide him over to assimilation by and within that collective human organism thrown together in random premeditation and the festive convention of organized disorder.

A party.

Well, be a party to it.

Or else, get out.

Was Al Lehman assimilable by this party? Or was he a lump unsmoothable over?

He's looked at, stared at. He averts that sea of faces.

His embarrassment is noticed.

He's bleeding from the deepest social wound. It stains the party, to the violent blush of red.

LV. POLITICAL PLIABILITY

Comes the revolution, and a new political regime will take over. Some heads will roll, but not Al Lehman's. He's always on the side that's in power, with which he identifies no matter which faction it is that currently is wielding it.

He's made up his personality of political patchwork quilt, to incorporate within himself an assimilated condensation of each party, movement, force, bloc, ideology, whatever. It's like receiving injections of immunity to each and every possible disease in advance. Thus, politically, anything can refer back to himself, and find preparation, loyalty, allegiance, to whatever the new reign or regime, however new the administration is: there's a chord of recognition already, for it, in Al Lehman. So he plays the current favorite, and follows wherever the popular trend will lead, having anticipated it well in advance by having covered all fields, every corner, leaving no stone of possibility to collect unturned dew.

He's so thoroughly all-political in bipartisanship unilaterally within each neutral zone, as to amount, practically, to being only apolitical. Thus the crucial center of balance rests nowhere in particular.

That's how he votes, too: by consensus. Popularity finds him foremost, in the solid pack.

Where does he *stand*, though? What are his firm principles and beliefs?

Everywhere and all of them. Or (much the same), nowhere and none.

He rides where history will lead. He's topically constant, in every flexible change of course. Disposed to espouse the latest power, with the pliable conviction of his all-seeing heart that stands for expedient self-interest at its pivotal core.

LVI. A SERIOUS RADIO PROGRAM, AND THE WRONG GUEST WHO SPOILS IT AND ALMOST RUINS THE SERIOUS CAREER AMBITIONS OF THE INTERVIEWER.

"In Capitalism, one man exploits another. In Communism, it's the other way around."

That was Al Lehman's reply, in a radio interview, to the question, "What are your political beliefs?" The interviewer was aghast. Such levity reflected a failure of political conviction. This was a serious program: its audience was known to be serious-minded: to take current world problems seriously.

In view of this, why had Al Lehman been given the honor of being invited onto the program, as a talking guest? Because he had been confused with another Al Lehman, who was an old man who at one time had been "behind the scenes" in local politics.

The radio station had phoned the "wrong" Al Lehman, in the mistaken belief that he was the "right" Al Lehman. When the wrong Al Lehman arrived at the appointed hour to the broadcasting studio, for the "live" broadcast, untaped, it was of course too late to rectify the mistake. The audience had not been told who the guest would be, so the announcer didn't have to explain about the mistake or to justify it. He just exaggerated some things about the identity of the Al Lehman who had turned up, making his job seen more important than it was, and making the guest into something of a "behind the scenes" political figure, active but unpublicized—all of this untrue, except being unpublicized.

But Al Lehman didn't cooperate, in the untruth. He made a public mockery of the program, and reduced the professional dignity of the interviewer with farcical answers to serious questions. Nor was he even well-intentioned. He delighted in prank to sabotage the show, to disgrace the interviewer, to ridicule the nature of that program. Perhaps the radio station would even remove the program altogether from the air, ruining the interviewer's incomplete career before he had become sufficiently a celebrity to get another esteemed job in broadcasting or graduate, even, to television itself, a field far more exalted.

So as soon as the program was ended, and they were safely "off the air," the interviewer, who had held himself back during the show, now let himself go, to the point of a punch to Al Lehman's jaw, which was neatly dodged. The studio engineers separated the two men. Al Lehman found an exit, and used it. He was gone. The interviewer was seething. A station executive assured the interviewer of retention of his precious job. The show would go on. Make sure to get the right guest, for next week's show. It was a vote of confidence. The interviewer was relieved. It was his big break. Now, his career would surge ahead. He saw a television future, yet. He'd survived the Al Lehman confusion. He was doubly bent, now, on success. He'd take off, to true greatness.

Next day, Al Lehman bought all the newspapers for their radio review columns. None made mention of the program he appeared on. He'll resume his anonymity, now, as a private person, relieved from public exposure. He retires, into his own life.

But his own life *includes* that radio appearance. His family, friends, colleagues, acquaintances, had all "enjoyed" the show. They appreciated his humor, his freedom from political solemnity, his light satire, and his belittling of the interviewer. In his own small, loose little connection bands, he was, of sorts, a local hero: a personality, who had bombarded radio, made a shambles of a "serious program," and come back to be the same old Al Lehman as before: his head unswollen, unturned, by his triumph over an ambitious interviewer who was now determined to leave that incident far behind, to become, later, a conversation or gossip piece, after his fame in television is long assured.

So the future dust settles, on those two men. Their slight scrape behind them, they go their separate ways, unlikely to mingle again in the dark chance course of combined incidental accident that fuses stray lives to one random current.

LVII. EXPOSING ONE'S LACK OF IDENTITY ON NATION-WIDE TELEVISION ON PRIME TIME, CAUSING THE STAR INTERVIEWER TO RETIRE FROM HIS EXALTED CELEBRITYHOOD INTO THE SAME OBSCURITY THAT THE GUEST HE INTERVIEWED EMERGED FROM AND RETURNED TO, ON THAT ILL-FATED PROGRAM.

"I have a different consciousness than someone who's a successful out-and-out businessman. Or than someone who's a virtuoso in the art of striking a pure belief in God. Or than someone for whom politics is more than what you merely read in the newspaper about it. Or than someone who gives deeply into the management of his family life."

"True enough, Al Lehman. But tell everyone in our national television audience on this interview show who you actually are in your own identity."

"*What* identity?"

"*Yours*, of course. Who else's?"

"No-one's but my own? My very own?"

"That's precisely what I'm endeavoring to get you widely to reveal, to expose outwardly, and to explode all theories to the contrary of. The identity you're protecting, under the guise of one of your well-known assumptions."

"But why would anyone. . ."

"You've struck the core of the national curiosity. That's why you're on this talk-show, in full view and well-engineered sound of a million identical strangers, or multi-millions, who are literally glued to this network channel for the sole hope of finding out, Al Lehman, just who you at all are, in the deepest and most inward recess of your full, direct, and manly being."

"It's hard to explain."

"Try."

"Well, being me is not always the picnic that a secret admirer can build it up enviously to be."

"I'm not asking how it's not; I'm asking *what* it *is*."

"What *what* is?"

"The *you*-ness, underneath all the *apparent* yous that you well-protectively assume."

"The me? It's in a process of becoming."

"Yes, but stamp a label on it, affix a definite definition to it."

"How can I? It's in flux."

"Then are you saying. . ."

"Correct, interviewer. That's what I'm *precisely* saying. That there *is no* definition to me. I'm possessed, as yet, of no known identity by which, either to myself or to others, I may come under the semblance of an identity."

"What you've said will come, undoubtedly, as something in the nature of a disappointment to this program's nation-wide attenders on private living-room sets all up and down the entire breadth and utmost mean average extent of this indivisible nation of ours. I've failed, as an interviewer, to get the real lowdown, the honest photojournalistic report, as to the true you of you. Therefore, I tender my resignation. As of this very instant."

"Don't: you're famous. *Far* more famous than *I*, in my modest guest appearance on this show, could ever hope—handicapped by my revealed lack of identity—to at all be. 'Be' is what I don't. I don't 'be.' "

"Yes, but why not? Al Lehman, tell the folks looking and listening in. Tell them, Al, *precisely*, why."

"Why *what*?"

"Why you don't be."

"*I* don't know. It's in my nature, I guess."

"What's in your nature?"

"This not-being business."

"You're wasting prime national television time, telling us that?"

"That's my statement, in summing up. It amounts to my self-assessment, such as it may be."

"This was the worst show I've ever professionally conducted, as my reputation goes plummeting down, in full view, in the sordid hour of my disgrace, before an appalled audience that tuned me in but who now bitterly regret it. I tender my resignation. I quit."

"But I'm not qualified to either receive or pass on your resignation. I'm only Al Lehman—your last guest."

"That's your identity—my last guest."

"Oh. So *that*'s what I am."

"Yes. Now, all is revealed."

End of television fiasco. Al Lehman was never asked to appear again on that popular medium. And the star interviewer, that celebrity, permanently retired from the scene. He lives, now, unidentified, in incognito. He's become as obscure as Al Lehman. Veiled, from all publicity, darkened in an utter void of limelight.

Secretly, he blames Al Lehman for his eclipse, his professional entertainment demise. *Openly* he does, too.

But openly and secretly are the same. There's no public to witness his privacy. He's become, virtually, an unknown. Stripped of his nationally established status of star glitter.

Al Lehman remains unaffected by all this perverse publicity. He goes on not having an identity. Even outside the overlit television studio. Even to his private audience, of one.

LVIII. A GREAT PHOTOGRAPHER'S LIFE PHO-TOGRAPH. HOWEVER, IT WASN'T TAKEN. SO HE WASN'T GREAT, NOR WAS HE A PHOTOGRAPHER. HOW FATAL, FOR THAT CAREER.

Briefly, Al Lehman, in his experimental choice of career, flirted with photography as a vocation, half for giving vent to an "artis-tic" nature, and half for its solid and reputable social accep-tance though hinting broadly nonetheless of a romantic bo-hemian sinister aspect allied darkly to that free category, "art."

But he couldn't make a living at it. There were already many veteran professionals out of work, newspapers and magazines having reduced their staffs or, in some cases, disappeared from circulation by ceasing publication altogether.

If he couldn't be a *commercial* photographer, then at least—or rather at most—why not be a pure genuine creative one with inspired technique to exalt the craft to the visual poetry of a fine art?

Eventually, his work would be exhibited in museums, by route first of increasingly well ranked art galleries.

Such fame and immortality pitched Al Lehman to ambi-tion's foremost star. All very well thus so ideally to dream. But had he the talent? Not skill alone, but such original vision as se-riously to claim that lofty due of a *genius*?

Frankly, no. Alas, that such negation should snuff out the rare glow of a promise he didn't have. Sad loss. But how loss, if he never had it?. Loss only to an illusion. An illusion which, by self-discovery, becomes its own loss.

He had envisaged an art publisher doing a whole "album" of his life's work that had by then already become so well known that the book of his collected photos merely confirmed the closing honor to crown culmination upon the accumulated monument to itself constituted by his collected photos of a lifetime, an illuminated retrospective in such complete depth that all the many photos from all the many series in his total phases of development all group themselves together and become, finally, simply one composite photograph of unspeakable grandeur in sweeping compass, uttering everything visible at a stroke. "A Photographer's Life Photograph," it should be called. A revelation of the world as revealed to Al Lehman, apostlyptic, showering legend and myth on mere material history.

But he hadn't the talent for it. Down the drain. A brilliant career, ruined, by what? He wasn't cut out for it. His eye was dull and dead: disastrous, for photographic immortality.

LIX. THE BUSINESS MAN ART COLLECTOR WHO
BEAUTIFIES MONEY AND FINANCES BEAUTY,
UNIFYING THOSE LONGSTANDING ENEMIES BY
AMASSING AN ACQUISITIVE EMPIRE OF SPECU-
LATIVE ART WEALTH AS A PERSONAL PROPERTY,
LIKE ANY OTHER UTILITY, THUS DESPOILING NA-
TURE OF ITS RICH NATURAL BOUNTY.

"All that money concentrated in all that beauty," admired the
art collector, who loved money for its own pure sake, accepting
beauty as a necessary evil which must be tolerated since, God
knows why, so much money could be condensed within a valuable work of art!

The art collector was a busy business man who really had
no time for art, so he hired guides, consultants, advisers, as
to which art should be bought, in speculation of appreciating
value.

Here he was, in a museum, looking at old masters hung
in gilded frames on walls, and exclaiming, out loud, "All that
money concentrated in all that beauty!"

Al Lehman, unemployed and dangerously "out of pocket"
in the depletion of his private funds, was standing near-by and
overheard it.

The businessman was a stranger, but Al Lehman was desperate. There was an economic recession, and he had wife
Marge and son Gregory to support, as well as his own eating self.

So he tried to convert this casual episode into a job opportunity. They were in a public place, but it was legal to begin conversation.

The business man looked obviously wealthy. Here was a
chance, for Al Lehman, bold and venturing, to acquire, per-

chance, a job, by striking up a conversation with this man of great means who has just exclaimed, out loud, in the public museum, in front of old masters, for anyone to overhear (and Al Lehman *was* the anyone who overheard), "All that money concentrated in all that beauty!"

Such a provocative uttered-out-loud-in-public statement mustn't go unanswered, for it represented the rarest of opportunities, if worked to profitable advantage. The moment was ripe or would be forever lost. Wit must be employed, but fast.

"Sir, you look like a collector," cagily began Al Lehman. "Well, I'm out of a job, and I offer you up services, for commission, fee, or on salary basis, of helping you, in your almighty busy-ness which makes you ill spare the time, to find, select, and purchase the highest quality works of art (prospectively-increasing in value) for your grand and ongrowing collection. Let me be the refined eye, for your acquisitive genius."

The business man was, indeed, highly impressed, by the stranger's correct assessment of himself as a busy business man who collects art as a profitable hobby or sideline but who can ill spare the time for such comparatively frivolous endeavors that ultimately would command high financial rewards.

"You're hired," he said, on the spot. Al Lehman beamed. Then the business man added, with a note of caution, "However, how qualified are you? If you were greatly qualified, then why, now, are you so profoundly out of a job?"

This slippery question caught Al Lehman surprised. But he recovered, and came out with a cunning reply, which seemed to allay the suspicions of this crafty business man.

So they came to terms. First on a trial basis, Al Lehman would have to show his worth, and prove his value.

✳

"I recommend this, this, that, this, to add to your collection," Al Lehman advised his new boss.

"Are they that beautiful? More importantly, will, by my keeping them, their value price go skyrocketing up in rise, so that later they'll be worth infinitely more than the lot that already now they're priced at?"

"That's my considered opinion, sir, if I so may venture, sir, a guess, which, in fact, is what you're paying me for, right? Right. So I advise you to buy. Then buy."

"Very well, then. I *will* buy."

"That's a smart boss. You have the brains to do what I recommend. You're too busy in your real business affairs to bother studying the art field and comparing aesthetic and monetary values of various works of art on potential sale to your collection. That's *my* job. Your collection is becoming a vast empire, and upon your death will become whole museums in themselves, thanks to my freedom with your wisely spending purse. Your name already strides the art world like a colossus in Midas gold. I'm making your fame even *more* wide-flung than that. With me as the scheming brains behind your collection, you'll own art itself, not just separate *works* of art. What a racket, and just for a sideline. As your shrewd chancellor of what to buy, I'm cornering the art market for you, and not just a slice of it, for your own private monopoly, like an electricity, gas, or transportation utility corporately controlled."

"Thanks, Al Lehman. Now you're fired."

"But why, boss? We're not done completing your collection yet, there's lots of deals a-brewing, with irons in the fire and merchant ships plying the seas of trade. We can't quit *now*.

We're giants in the building process, just now, for accumulating, acquiring, on an all-but-ruthless scale. Why pull out *now*? A little more spending, in crucial places, will bring enormous art fortune our way. We can't trim our sails when the winds blow auspiciously and the seas plow an enterprising route in the tides of our favor. So what gives? You're only joking, for sure?"

"No, Al Lehman, I'm too sincere to be funny. I've gotten religion, you see? So I'm not going to exploit art or beauty for money's sake, amassing personal gain by tricky practice. I'm giving up being a business man, *and* a collector. I'm devoting myself to religion, with a new emphasis against material acquisition, all that vulgar hoarding in corrupt exchange. I'm returning the art to the people, and breaking up my collection, going austere. I can't afford you any more. You're a vicious reminder of my past. Spirituality is my new game. You're not fit for it. I've tided you over in an economic recession. Now your wife Marge and son Gregory eat well and you're reasonably secure for a while, having salted away a tidy sum earned as my art administrator. For a while, you're on easy street, eased of worry. Now, I cut you off from my employ; out *you* go, and up *I* go, to God in a moneyless heaven, where beauty isn't possessed as legal pillage and plunder, but prized in the *mind*. I renounce all that I did, including what you helped me do. Beauty should be a moneyless commodity—or rather, not a commodity at all. Beauty belongs to God and man. I'm going to purify it of commercial taint. Man-made beauty is art. Natural beauty is nature's. They're free. In God."

LX. ART MISTAKENLY SLIGHTED TO THE SPECIF-
ICALLY WRONG PERSON AT A GALLERY OPEN-
ING TO CELEBRATE THE EXHIBIT; AND ITS SWIFT
REPERCUSSIONS THAT COMPOUND OFFENSIVE
ERROR WITH INJURIOUS RETALIATION IN A VIO-
LENT INCIDENT. THEN THE HARM IS SWALLOWED
UP BY A DOUBLE GULP OF OBLIVION, TWO MEM-
ORIES FORGETTING SEPARATE VERSIONS, WHILE
UNITED TO THEIR COMMON ROUTE THAT WEEDS
OUT DIFFERENCES IN DEATH'S ULTIMATE DIVI-
SION, THE GALLERY-CLOSING FOR IMPERSONAL
GUESTS, WHERE ART IS RULED OUT AS A JOINER
OF TASTE COLLISIONS.

Here he was, at an art gallery opening: people drinking and talking; paintings hung on walls. Al Lehman didn't know the artist,
but what did that matter? He knew one or two other guests, but
did most of his talking with strangers. He was getting drunk.

He went over to the bottle table to refuel his by now de-
pleted glass. A stranger was doing likewise, and their bodies
accidentally tangled. To cover the momentary embarrassment
with the social-poise-restorative of conversation, Al Lehman
gestured sweepingly at a painting-cluttered wall with semi-
drunken lunge, as though broadly to condemn the whole artis-
tic display into one easily dismissed lump too lightly regarded
to merit the serious consideration implicit within perverse esteem of contempt.

When the gesture was completed, Al Lehman punctuated
his impromptu mime with these words to the same effect:
"What do *you* think of this so-called art? Is it even worth an
opinion?"

The stranger, at first, didn't answer. Fury crinkled at his face. Rage burned in his glare. He stared headlong into Al Lehman's startled eyes that crumbled into contrite submission.

The message was now dawning on Al Lehman, as the tactless blunder of his faux pas was taking cruel vengeance on the unwitting perpetrator, now shrunk and shriveled into a puny war between weak-kneed remorse and repentance-resistant pride, on an ill-lit stage of his own anguished interior drama.

Al Lehman blurted out: "Actually, I was only fooling. I greatly admire your paintings. It's a fascinating exhibit."

Next followed a punch in the jaw by the artist, a fine non-brushwork stroke, which had a telling effect on Al Lehman's consciousness by momentarily dimming it out. From the force of the blow, Al Lehman's large body was propelled backward. A leg scraped the bottle table and overturned some vacated glasses with only dregs left in them in near-emptiness. His head went through a canvas, crashed against the wooden wall behind it, and then slumped forward to the chest, as the body sagged and crumbled to the floor. A local sensation ensued. Gallery guests were shocked, but entertained.

It was the high point, of that well-attended opening. Few people knew Al Lehman, so the disgrace to his reputation didn't endure thereafter.

He never ever encountered that artist again. One time proved to have been sufficient for at least their two lifetimes.

It had been an uneasy incident. Awkward, and, if possible, forgettable.

From two offended points of view.

The artist and Al Lehman are eternally allied. Their bond is firmer than quite a few friendships. Aesthetic division holds them fast. Discord, by several decisive acts, in a swift eventful sequence.

A difference of taste had been exchanged, with tasteless promptness, that included a discovery scene and violence by the wounded party.

All in art's fair name. Brutal words—unintended personally—and a direct deed by retaliation.

End of the art gallery opening. The paintings sold well. The artist is almost famous. Al Lehman isn't. Their "fates" diverge. From one intimate—but impersonal—incident.

Years go by. The two men are aging. Toward separate ends.

They converge, to the same division. From one abrupt clash, to their soft, impersonal union, their common discharge of a mortal mutual debt; along with all the countless others never once brought together by an occasion of art, a public commercial event by invitation including the crashers. An addition by two, to an eternal drift.

The universe is a work of human art. Its gaping imperfections mar life, and blot its peace.

Farewell Al Lehman, and the artist. In time and place they overlapped, by city and generation. Their matters now are mixed. As ever their opinions were.

In a drunk scene, and an unrecognized identity. It vividly occurred once. Violently, it was over. The elements had combined. A compounded mistake. A fierce collision.

Then two lives, resumed. By passages well apart. Dark and lit, by turns, on separate ways, independent consciousnesses. Each with social trimmings, and cluttered loneliness.

Two men. One event. Two deaths. Succeeded by one old popular nothingness, to blot their cases equal, stamped for the inactive file, and filed away forgotten by fresh born takers-over of the city's changing face. The planet's high city where an art world can take place. Earth paved for local commerce on a universal plane. Ideals of sophisticated society. Fortune-seeking art, in the glitter of drink and fame.

LXI. AN ART MUSEUM BEFORE IT WAS BUILT, BEFORE ITS WORKS WERE COLLECTED AND IN- STALLED, BEFORE IT WAS STAFFED, OR OPEN TO THE PUBLIC. AL LEHMAN'S PREMATURE VISIT TO IT. A PRANK, OR QUIRK, IN THE UNIQUE ANNALS OF TIME. THE CRAZY PRIVATE—UNPUBLICLY- ADMITTED. THE SECRET FROM SOCIETY. KEPT UNTOLD, AS UNLIKELY FANTASY, UNTIL NOW: UN- TIL THIS STORY REPORTS IT. THE STORY YOU READ, HERE.

Al Lehman went to a museum before it was even built. This was an odd trick of time. In fact, the paintings hadn't even been ac- quired yet.

Yet, there Al Lehman was. On the front steps, then through the entrance framed by portico columns. Into the vast lobby, or foyer. Past the admissions booth. Into galleries echoing with col- lections of grand masters of all the periods of every nation.

He made a trip to the bathroom, which additionally served to break up the unrelieved immersion in such a profuse abun- dance of man-made artificial grand aesthetics.

The guards were there, but as yet no member of the public, since the museum was yet to be built, the art collections yet to be acquired. How did Al Lehman get to be so premature and yet so actual, in there?

Time was meant for all people in common. But in this case, here was Al Lehman being an exception. He preceded all other museum visitors.

But how were the paintings, walls, guards, floors, stairs, sculpture, bathroom, and other things there, for Al Lehman to prematurely see, before they were *publicly* there for the general open public to see and use and be among and walk through? Time, here, was playing favorites. It was indulging Al Lehman's prematurity.

Why *him*? And anyway, why and how *anyone*? By what method did time work this miracle?

The secret is not revealed. So the event just has to be accepted: Al Lehman's visit to a pre-built museum, enjoying art pre-acquired by that museum.

The space that the museum was to occupy was a grass-and-tree area in a big public park. The public was using that park space to stroll through or sit in, at the same "time" that Al Lehman was in the museum *later* built there.

There suffices that there's no explanation. Al Lehman came to be privileged, but no-one else.

Now the museum is officially built, open to the public, its exhibits on display.

Al Lehman pays a new visit, along with a crowd of other visitors—real people.

So too is Al Lehman real. *Was* he real the *first* time he came here?

He *must* have been, for he remembers the visit. A more unique experience could be hard to imagine.

Or was it a unique imagining, that he experienced?

Words shouldn't be quibbled with, here. What's at stake is reality, time, experience, and suchlike matters, all equally unfrivolous.

Who's to believe Al Lehman? No-one *has* to, for he's told no-one. Why submit them, to such an unlikely test? It's unfair, to their credulity, to their common-sense, even to their self-respect.

No-one knows. Nevertheless, here's the story of it.

A quirk in time? A hallucination by Al Lehman, under the spell of some extraordinary illusion?

It's *easy* to visit a museum after it's been built, supplied with art, staffed, and readied for the public-at-large.

Al Lehman, though, did the *hard* thing. *Unbelievably* hard.

No-one knew; but now the story's out—this account of it.

What will it prove?

Stories are often fantasies. They're not to be accounted, as historical documents that would verify actual phenomena gone by.

Al Lehman is all alone. All alone, with this single memory. Does *he* even believe it? *Can* he even believe it?—For it's unshared.

Sharing makes something uncrazy. Sharing is confirming. And that's belief.

Terribly, tediously alone. To be self-suspicious, of a museum visit among other, creditable experiences.

The past is in the dark. It's outside certifiable visibility.

In his *recent* public-shared visit to the same museum, Al Lehman recognized the same paintings he had "seen before"—within those very walls. He even recognized the same guards. He had been there before.

He most certainly had been there before. Most definitely, he had. Indisputably, he had.

All alone. But the conviction is fading: with no-one to endorse it, to back it up.

Hogwash, fantasy, baloney. Sheer rubbish. Utter nonsense.

Al Lehman denies it, to his critical self.

Denial accepted.

Welcome back to the human race. To sane humanity, at large. To the museum-flowing crowd. In with them, joining their own time. Time's common property. Unifying all adventures, in a sane frame of reference. Your events acceptable to the rest, taking on a joint property, a social sanction of a sharing. What belongs to you belongs to all; and so do you. You submit your experiences to the board of inspection. In the human art museum, join the collection.

LXII. ALLERGY TO ART: ITS DIFFICULT CURE

One of Al Lehman's "psychology" patients had a strange allergy: to art, of all things. He'd sneeze and cough—violently—if exposed to a masterpiece; gently, if exposed to some lesser work of art.

Al Lehman was unable, at first, to account for his patient's— to put it mildly—unusual condition. But with repeated sessions, they'd hammer away at some sort of "depth" explanation.

"Were you ever injured by a work of art during your pre- or post-embryonic early infancy?"

"Not that I can remember."

"Your lack of recall is holding up our analysis, and depriving us of essential insight."

"But I was too young, at the time, to form memorable impressions," the patient sobbed, wishing his psychologist would be more patient and understanding.

Instead, Al Lehman snapped, "Why are you so hostile to art?"

This outburst of uncontrolled anger gave the patient a nervous breakdown, on the spot, complete with hysteria, rage, repression, and hallucinatory delusions. "We're getting close to the answer," Al Lehman shouted, warming up to his professional difficulty, willing to undertake a challenge that would daunt his lesser colleagues.

The patient, however, couldn't share in Al Lehman's warmhearted enthusiasm. Instead, he succumbed to semi-collapse, displaying classical symptoms of catatonic stupor, which Al Lehman gleefully noted, the sleuth sensing the kill, the hunter his quarry, the inventor his discovery, the scientific dog his ultimate investigative scent.

"Maybe I wasn't gentle enough," mused Al Lehman, now that his patient, rather than recovering, had slumped into a rather alarming coma. "We can't continue the analysis, with him so vegetable-like. I must get him to a hospital, to a ward whose walls are devoid of works of art, even reproduction copies, so that his allergy wouldn't be continually exposed, activated, and recharged."

On the way to the hospital, the patient died. A thorough investigation started. The last few hours of the dead man's life had taken place in Al Lehman's psychology office. The authorities subjected Al Lehman to a merciless grilling, round after round of questioning. It was possible that Al Lehman would be accused of indirect murder through malpractice—a dreadfully serious charge by which his license for practicing psychology would be canceled, and his short-lived career broken off at its virtual root.

How he acquitted himself under intensive questioning was crucial in another way beside preserving his profession: avoidance of a jail term which would entail character-degrading consequences that would radically alter his life for the worse, with disastrous results for whatever social standing he esteemed himself eminent of.

The prosecuting attorney asked the defendant questions about art and therapy, allergy and psychology, therapeutic methods and procedures, art and repression, art and ego, psychosomatic illness and art, hysteria and art, and other allied or related subjects. Al Lehman handled them all well, and eventually was acquitted, retaining his license, with only a mild cautioning by the magistrate about leniency as opposed to severity in handling a touchy patient whose nerves were out of kilter with social rhythm and required delicacy of approach, even gentle coddling, to sooth an ego bruised and battered by a world ambivalently murderous in its religious awe toward art.

"I got off easy, I feel great relief," rejoiced Al Lehman, leaving court. However, as he descended to the bottom step outside the phony Roman building, a bullet-shot nipped his arm and drew blood. Luckily, police were there, and they wrestled the shooter down before a more lethal shot could be fired. It proved to be the bereaved wife of Al Lehman's art-allergic patient, or ex-patient and current corpse.

"That was close," sang out Al Lehman, after his superficial wound was attended to. "But she may get off after a light sentence and look for me again with murderous intent to avenge the husband I've caused her to mourn for. It's hanging over me, this insecurity. Maybe I'll move out of town, to escape that possibility. I'm divorced and my kid is out of town anyway, though of course my profession and roots are here, my possessions, collections, friends, relatives, all that.

"So I'll brave it out, and stay. But that grief-crazed wife of my former art-allergic patient would constitute a constant sort of danger. I must make some sort of pact with her. She's young and pretty, so I'll marry her. That way, in her proxy, I'll continue posthumous therapy on her deranged husband, finally to solve why he sneezes and coughs when exposed to works of art. A romantic conclusion, to a knotty problem."

LXIII. AL LEHMAN GETS INTO A DIALOGUE WITH SOMEONE WHO WANTS TO TALK ABOUT A FOG. THE LATTER SPEAKS FIRST, THEN AL LEHMAN ANSWERS, AND SO ON IN ALTERNATION. THE FOG REMAINS, AS THE THIRD CHARACTER, BUT—SO AS NOT TO CLOUD THE ISSUE—A SILENT ONE.

If I'm talking about a fog, should I speak clearly?

No, for then you would obscure your subject.

But am I clouding the issue by treating my subject in a fog-like manner, fitting form to content, shape to theme, style to topic?

No, you shed rays of illumination on the fog, its particular nature, its peculiar essence.

Then I'd *dispel* the fog; for in clarifying it, I clear it out from what it is.

If you write in a dull and overhanging way, you keep closer fidelity to what you write of?

Yes. I was only going to *talk* about the fog; now I'll write of it. Why?

The writing will remain longer. The talk evaporates in air. But words written down linger.

And the fog they treat of will linger too.

Yes—but just in a manner of speaking.

Such airy matter, in such containing manner.

LXIV. THE PARADOX THAT ALMOST BECAME UN-EXPLAINED

"Some things that I hate, I like better than some things that I like," Al Lehman remarked, leaving the paradox unspecified. He told this to the poet, who was unsatisfied at it being left like that, and demanded an example. or several.

Al Lehman was brought up short. "I can't think of any," he confessed, after deliberating, pondering, reflecting, meditating, contemplating, cogitating, and suchlike activities involving the cerebellum, an inner part of the head that was an improved version on the standard of the early mammal model.

Such activities made no noise, so the poet sat quietly while Al Lehman underwent them. Soon, however, the poet got bored, listening to nothing. (Anyone would. What has "nothing" to offer? Very little, if anything at all.)

"Then why did you say it?" the poet asked, eventually, when the silence was making too much of itself and stopping anything else from happening.

"Say what?" asked Al Lehman, distracted from his own forgetting, and caught up in the coils of thought that had abstracted itself out of content, substance, matter, subject, or whatever gives impetus, ballast, leverage, and force to thinking, as such.

"Let me quote you," the poet reminded Al Lehman: " 'Some things that I hate, I like better than some things that I like.' That's what you said, but when I asked you to illustrate with examples, you thought for a while, and seemed to be at a loss."

"Can't we leave it unspecified?" asked Al Lehman. "Can't we just leave it at that? Can't you read in your *own* examples, if you want to deck out my vague generality in any concrete particular?"

"No, it's up to *you* to finish what you started."

"I already finished it, by saying what I did. It left *you* unsatisfied, not me."

All Lehman said that sharply. The poet looked crestfallen. Then Al Lehman softened up: "I hate this kind of conversation with you; but I like it better than some things that I like," Al Lehman specified, with an example right at hand. Thus, their whole conversation was the illustration of what began it. It was complete, self-sufficient, this talk or argument that grew its own form from its general opening paradox, took shape upon it, and ended by providing some actual body of concrete experience by which it all rolled together as an entity, in its own right, basing existence on what had been said, from opening statement, through pauses and replies, and to the revelation that left nothing to be added, within the being that had been established by Al Lehman's talk with his poet. There, the matter ended, all embodied as a form that had taken place, through thought exchanges on the silent scroll of worded time.

LXV. IS YAWNING A TIRED ACT?

During a conversation, Al Lehman was told this by someone:

"I was too tired to yawn."

"But when you're in the mood, yawning can be so easy!"

"But I was so tired, that even opening my mouth was a chore, laborious, an effort, a task."

"It doesn't require very much energy: being tired even makes it *easy* to open the mouth. In fact, when you're *really* tired, it's difficult *not* to open the mouth. Let me demonstrate."

"Yes, I see that your mouth is open, but how do I know that you're really tired? You look like you're only playing a game, just acting."

"Trust me. I'm Al Lehman."

"Of *course* you're Al lehman. Have you ever been anyone else?"

"No; my whole life is given over to being him; it's a full-time effort, I can tell you. Have you ever tried it?"

"No; I have my hands full, just being myself all life long."

"Now you know what *I* have to go through."

"I can well imagine. But it must be fun, at times, as well."

"I must admit, frankly, that being Al Lehman has its light moments, and, what's more, can offer up surprising consolation, at times."

"What do you need to be consoled for?"

"*You* ought to know. You may not be Al Lehman, as only I am, but you have your *own* life to live; and that can give you a clue."

"It's the *waking* part of life that troubles me. Is that so in *your* case?"

"Perfectly so. It's *everyone's* problem, I think."

That ended the conversation, between Al Lehman and the other man. As for *who* the other man was, his identity was limited to being one of the non-Al Lehmans of this world: those whom Al Lehman would refer to as "others," as distinct from him*self.*

Him*self,* he was in full. No-one was even that in *part,* or even in *degree,* let alone *kind.*

Still, there were areas of common interest, bonds and barriers of talk. All the theys, and the he.

The other man was gone, and Al Lehman rankled. The other hadn't believed Al Lehman's sincerity in demonstrating the difficulty of not opening the mouth while yawning, or some such technical expression of tiredness through yawning's outlet while not being any less tired for the exercise. Al Lehman had been accused of only pretending to be tired, thus nulling and voiding the truth of his physical demonstration via an open mouth.

Too late to protest. But *had* he really been tired? It was so easy to forget whether he had been, in spite of which, he remembered that he had not been.

He had dishonestly represented himself. Identity is such a chore. He was awfully tired, by now. His mouth was glum, and closed.

LXVI. SWEARING'S PRECURSORS

Before swearing ever began, there were the *precursors* of that art. This original foul language has come cursing down to us with a tradition. So when Al Lehman swears, he stands before a lot behind him, a whole linguistry of words boiled in hell's temperature, coined to the vat of the infernal mint, before rolling off his lips in cosy oaths, perfectly acceptable today.

LXVII. CHEAPLY BEING UNDERSTOOD, OR FULLY BEING MISUNDERSTOOD? DEPTHS OF COMMUNICATION, THE LEVELS OF AUDIENCE.

"Life is a continuum modified by continual discontinuities," Al Lehman was quick to point out. His point, however, was lost, on his many misunderstanders. So he said it again, slowly, giving the point, this time, time to sink in.

However, his misunderstanders had gone away, reducing his audience to nil. At least, that way, his being misunderstood was kept to its utter and absolute minimum.

But he yearned to be understood. Next time, when he had some listeners in front of him, he'd try something different to tell them.

Something, perhaps, more continuous? Easier to follow? With some line of development? Simplified, pared down, pruned away, to a harmless feat of logic?

That would compromise his ideas. He'd communicate on paper, then: to an unseen audience, ideally lettered.

The full idea transmitted fully, understood fully, by a universal brotherhood of "others": whom he'd never know; but be known *by*. To the tune of understanding's eternal clang, the everlasting echo of its bell.

LXVIII. THOUGHT GETTING OUT OF HAND, UNRULY. IT TOOK AL LEHMAN IN HAND, AND RULED HIM. OR ANYWAY, THAT'S WHAT *HE* THOUGHT WAS GOING ON. BUT *THOUGHT* HAD ITS SAY, TOO. IT CAST HIM, IN ITS OWN IDEA.

Vacillating between religion and philosophy, caught somewhere between ontology's mountains and the wide open plains of metaphysics, Al Lehman kept thinking. Under those quite trying circumstances, he had no recourse but to think. After such exhaustions, he tried to stop thinking, but found, in bewilderment and alarm, that he was unable to. Thought was simply happening to him, and there seemed nothing he could do about it, having no power to arrest its incessant self-persistence that took on its own tyrannic autonomy and forced Al Lehman to be its mental receiving vessel, its own private carrier.

He couldn't shut it off. The thought was a continuous live jumping wave or beam, a sequential series of successivenesses in endless interpermeation. He was being used, a vehicle or conduit, by the wayward will of his onward thought.

This unprecedented predicament presented a problem that permitted no ready solution but could simply only be wondered at. Wondering was passive. Was the problem pathological? Then remedy must be resorted to. Yes, but where?

Meanwhile, his thought continued, like a plague or disease, unarrested, in the wild frolic of its career, surging or hurtling over him, or within him, like a cascade of torrential fury, a push of armed might in warlike attack (carrying to the enemy the well-co-ordinated brunt of offensive at, as it were, the enemy's own front doorstep, in forcing the pace).

Like a stampede of animals, Al Lehman's thoughts went whizzing by from a rear of endless reserve, like the disciplined charge of a brave brigade.

But wasn't he *meant* to think? He tried to rationalize his own thinking. Thinking was an inherent human faculty. It had to be put in use. It *insisted* on use. What use did it serve? It solved problems, theoretical, practical, actual, or reflective. But now it had *become* a problem. How could he employ it to moderate, abate, or resolve its own self?! Indeed, this *was* a problem!

What could he do? Thought was implicated in his doing. It wouldn't permit him to sabotage its own process. It sought self-perpetuation—despite his intention to subdue it, to puncture its swollen thrust, till it subsided and let itself be ruled by what *Al Lehman* would determine for itself and it.

But how could he determine *anything,* save by thought? This caught him up, in the fruitless repetition of a circle wherein futility struggled and was enclosed.

He wanted to stop thinking. That was what he *thought* he wanted. He was controlled by the thought of wanting to stop thinking. Thought had ordered him to think that he was thinking too much. Under its control, he tried to control it—but in vain. It bound him fast to its own internal device, and outwitted him at every turn. It commanded the machinery, and knew how to manipulate their capital assets. It held the cards including the trump card. He was under its spell. He was thought's tool. He articulated, to its every command. He did its bidding. It compelled even his resistance to it, which it quelled, by cynical ruthlessness. It was authoritarian to him, in total dictatorship. It provoked him to riot, which it promptly subdued. It tricked him into protest, which then it stamped out.

Under thought's tyranny, Al Lehman could only submit. It told him what to think. It suborned his facilities, and mobilized every brain cell he owned, to its own "national" interest.

Thought *was* himself. It governed, but the government and the governed were equally himself and it. He identified, then, with his master. It assimilated him, to their corporate wish, in league, together.

LXIX. IN THE BLACK TUNNEL

The night wore on, darker and darker. Al Lehman was walking to the end of his troubles, through the winding tunnel of all the misery that had totalled up from wretched moments that his lifetime had to suffer through, along with all the better feelings that lightened his many ways.

He seemed to be walking back into another era, though at the forward normal walking gait. There were blissful nostalgic patches of his past that he longed to re-attain, through some optimistic turn, a marvelous chance combining of habits and hopes and memories, favored by fortunate new circumstance, a new social occasion, the full flourish of every faculty he owned.

The night wore deep. On he trod. He was looking for heaven when the tunnel opened at the end; or just a glimpse; a new land in space; the ideal city; or the past perfected.

Through the night. Through time and sleep. Into another area, as well as era. Where it would be light. Where he'd feel better and control it. Where the social occasions, the sets of circumstance, fully fit in with his own best being.

But he was asleep? Alas, then he must wake.

And lose, and lose, by waking?

But how could he lose what he didn't have?

He *had* it: but in a tenuous dream. To be dissolved, upon mere waking.

But retained partially? Incompletely? To torture himself with? That he barely had it, whatever "it" was, by a bare mental string, a concept of his heart, which the world would deny and remain at odds with, and discourage his retaining, in his social moments ahead and his remote sad solitude, feeling *with-*

out? What is that "without"? He lacks, but what? Which deepest desire can't claim.

And the dream was fleeting. His tunnel stopped. He didn't see the light end, but he stopped before that. In the rich shroud of darkness. In vain longing. At ideal odds with this finite world grasping with social life, with sexual substitutes for love, with coveted glory in work, career, status, achievement, power, truth, whatever.

The commercially impure world, the popular social jungle, envious competition.

The tunnel stopped, before the light end.

Beyond? So there is one. But to be traversed? Entered? Seen? Not yet. Or will another night come—and the dream thrust further? That unassisted dream. A league removed, from suffering and tainted joy.

LXX. THAT ENDLESS SUBJECT, WORRY

"Without worry, we'd have been dead long ago. Worry keeps us on the alert. It alerts us, to be on our guard. By it, we're made responsible, to keep harm away. We look after ourselves. We look out for trouble.

"Worry shows apprehension of maybe trouble brewing. Something may be wrong, or *is* wrong, so worry broods what can be done, to conduct search toward a remedy. It looks for alleviation. It seeks to be solved: its own demise. Then worry's job is over, when it's moved us to undo itself, during its unpleasant existence in us."

This was Al Lehman's study on the importance of worry, its function and value in us. He submitted it to a journal of psychology, and by return mail received a letter of acceptance by the editor, accompanied by a check in payment. Space was made for this essay in the next issue, which was just about to go to press. Al Lehman was so honored, that he took psychology courses at a college, got his diploma, and took out a license to practice psychology on patients who either worry unduly or don't worry enough, depending on what the circumstances might be in each case. When to worry, and when not to, depend, of course, on what the worry is about, and what can be done, in what way, about what the worry is concerned with. The future is often unpredictable. What should we do? What *shouldn't* we do? What are the chances of this happening, or that? When should we leave things to chance? When should we take active steps, intervening, to alter things? What *is* alterable? When should we leave "well enough" alone, and how can we judge, size up, assess, the likelihood of this or that, in estimating what our moves should be, to prevent this, to avert that, to modify, to anticipate, get around, avoid, or instigate?

Worry concerns the future. Some dread is mingled in it, usually. It's so situational. We reflect and guess, as well as tap experience, to form calculation.

Al Lehman doesn't have to worry that he'll lose or stop gaining patients when there comes to be not enough things to worry about. His future is guaranteed. His expert services will always be needed, for consultation, advice, guidance, counseling. People are bound to worry. The world and other people make sure of that.

Al Lehman, then, has a secure living. Worry is his trade. Its natural resources are inexhaustible, within the peopled world of the uncertain future. Doubt always comes about. Don't worry. See Doctor Lehman. He'll tell you if you *ought* to worry, when, and how. And what *about*. He'll educate you, within inevitable limitations, about different unknowns that you have to wait for, and wait, before. . .

Before what? Ah, that's worry's business.

LXXI. A RATHER EVENTFUL WALK

Such a long walk Al Lehman took, that eventually he arrived somewhere where he had never been before. From that point on, as he continued walking, there was continuous unfamiliarity.

Even the very people themselves seemed different than any he had seen anywhere else before! They belonged to strange new races that had never been reported yet. They walked differently, talked differently, dressed differently—but not differently in the same way; differently in different ways.

The trees and plants were different, too. The buildings were different; the street layouts and avenue arrangements were different. Somehow, even, the sky seemed different. Canals and lakes he encountered were different too. All the scenery, and the animals, too. He was up against no cliche or stereotype. He was in a wonderful adventure, an absolutely pure experience, free from precedence or hackneyed similarity. This strangeness would strain him. The stress might prove too much for habit-reliant faculties. It was enchanting, now. Later, he could crack.

He had to check: was be dreaming? No. Going crazy? No, not yet. Did he happen to be in a foreign country? No, he had merely taken a long walk in his own. He had encountered a fabulous wonderland, of rich enchantment. Some magic glory. Or some wild terror?

He himself excited no curiosity on the part of these "natives." They acted as though he were ordinary enough, by ignoring him.

On *his* side, he was ignoring nothing. Everything, from small to large scale, just burst forth like a miracle. A well-paced drama of constantly varied shock assaulted his naked senses.

He paused from outside stimulation, to break the barrage, taking refuge within introspection. He examined his own credentials: he was still Al Lehman. He still had his own past. Yet, why all *this*, now?

Assured that he was himself, he resumed subjecting that self to this weirdness and incredibility around him.

He addressed himself to it. It was certifiable, and real. That this was taking place, before him, there was no doubt.

Yet, everything seemed normal enough, judging by the non-surprise of the "native" people here. Regular procedure seemed to be underway. Good. All this was typical, that was confronting him. It was all the more staggering, for that. The commonplace was occurring. That's quite amazing.

How long would this last? He was tired. He had walked, it seemed, right into another dimension; a walk much longer than anticipated, which had taken him quite into the unknown—literally, not metaphorically.

He sat down, on a kind of public bench (between a park square and a crowded street cross-section) that he had never conceived of before, much less looked at or sat on.

How much newness could he withstand? He began to long for the good old familiar.

At that, he was asleep. He dreamed he was back in the familiar—which, however, had become, meanwhile, unfamiliar.

Perhaps, he would *never* return to it—to find it unchanged. That was the dream's warning.

He woke up. He was approaching night.

He would soon start walking back.

But he might never get there! The tongues around him were unfamiliar. They couldn't direct him. He was lost.

He was stuck, here.

No; some official was sure to know his own language. He had, though, to consult the right one.

This was too adventurous. He wearied of it. "Comfort lies in the familiar," buzzed some voice.

It came from his own head. Who was he, where was he, and why? Even the "when" might be altered; even that!

How was he here? By walking a little too far; in, of course, this direction.

When he spoke, people ignored him and walked by. He felt absurd, out of place. Insubstantial, or phantasmal.

Was he even visible? Did his body carry weight?

It was spooky, eerie. He was chilly. It was unpleasant.

He was perhaps going crazy? No, all this was too real.

Wasn't he dreaming? No. This was too real.

Surely, this was a foreign country? But he had crossed no borderline, on that rather momentous walk that had led him to the improbability of his being here.

But where was he? He wanted to break into a scream. In fact, he did.

No-one appeared to hear. He was totally ignored.

"I must be dead," he thought. Then paused, to consider. "No, of course not. Death is *hardly* like this."

Yes, but what *is* like this? What, in the world, is?

He pondered. And now it was morning!

"It must be spring," he thought.

He walked, he tried to get back. Yes, but where *from*?

The scenes changed.

He kept walking.

He was so tired!

It got to be bright noon. It was sweaty and hot. He plodded on.

More strange scenes! *More!*

Will the unusual ever stop?!

Novelty after novelty. Each newness newer than before. Not one thing familiar.

Let this end! He'll go mad!

He's breaking down. His screams are ignored. No-one heeds him, nothing. Unseen, he's a thorough stranger, and unheard.

His bearings—where are they? Where's *any* comfort?

The customary, the unexceptional. All in order, regular and predictable. When will that state he resumed? In what context?

Not one reply, in or out. No steady answer, anywhere? No stability, no certainty. No firm, positive sense. No direction.

All was a "no." In this incredible "Yes."

LXXII. FISHING FOR LAKE TROUT ON A RENTED ROWBOAT; A JULY SATURDAY DEVOTED TO PEACE AND FORGETFULNESS; A SWEET AND RELIABLE ESCAPE FROM A HOME BROOD OF WORRIES.

Fishing in a trout lake, the sun gliding off, little circles skimming on the lake's surface before going still.

Birds darting among the clouds. A placid rowboat.

In it, Al Lehman, with his active fishing rod. Stirs and agitations, but not quite a nibble.

The boat is too small for him. The world is too wide for him. The lake too deep, the sky too high; the sun not quite warm enough, today.

At other days, the sun would sometimes be even *too* hot. It all evened out, when all the days piled up to be measured for an average mean. But who cared about that? The main thing, just now, was that, here he was, stagnantly afloat, oars inside, on the drifting middle of a lake, where ripples appeared and went; and on the surrounding shore the unmatching trees swayed in lazily uneven rhythm. And here he was, Al Lehman, big with his own body crammed into a too-small rowboat, bothered by cold weather.

He shivered, even shuddered, while the sun was ornamentally bright but coldly indifferent to an exposed man fishing on a lake of nature in technical July, unseasonable July, untrue to a tradition that promised gorgeous temperature.

His temperament was ruffled. He had family worries and job worries. Discord with his wife hinted at separation and divorce. Their little son would be caught in the middle, an undeserving victim of bickering malice between parents armed into warring strangers, bitterly wronged by each other's disputed injustice, the wrong atmosphere for a puzzled and torn son.

At the office, the current policy was to lay off (fire) some regular but vulnerable employees; Al Lehman's status, there, was precarious.

This July Saturday was to forget woes. A fishing respite, renting a rowboat, plying a lake layer-deep in trout that streamed in from a river with blazing rainbow coats.

A forgetful Saturday, in pleasurable ease.

Instead, his cares came sharply flocking in, just oozing with poison woe.

Not a nibble on his wormed hook.

Bubbles and gurgles, swift circles that die down.

The water was skipping with cold. As if in irony, the sun breasted itself out in a blinding blaze of turbulent visual frigidity, a broad hoax of glacial warmth-promise. A prank from the heavens, mocking the sole fisher.

Suicide by drowning? Don't be silly. You'd never have another chance to redeem yourself, damn fool, from these helpless circumstances.

He gave up fishing, put down the rod, picked up oars, rowed toward shore.

Well, he was taking action. He was improving his condition. Why be a victim? Nature hadn't cooperated: no biting fish, no mental peace of problem-forgetting, no warm comfort for all his great big body.

He'll be going home. Get to shore, turn in the rented rowboat to the owner's shack, walk to the parked car by the road's end; and drive back.

To an angry wife. To uncertain job security. To peril, ahead.

The sun snarled. Al Lehman obscenely gesticulated toward it. He returned his futile little rowboat, and walked toward his car, at the end of the road, brooding on all his plague of bothers.

Where his car should be, he found instead some smashed glass. Someone had knocked in a window to reach in and open the door from the inside; had stolen the car.

The sun was declining. Here he was, near the edge of a lake. Not in the best of moods, except for some exceptional self-pity.

What would he at all do? He returned to the rowboat-owner's shack, to phone the police, only to be told that the phone wasn't working, that the repairers would arrive some-time tomorrow.

A failed fishing expedition. He had hoped to step apart from his troubles. Now, in the chill, his predicament had heaped more misery on.

The rowboat owner was curtly unsympathetic. Al Lehman was advised to walk to town, to police, to a roughshod hotel. Not a warming prospect.

Religion and philosophy would be referred to. Worldly mat-ters hadn't availed, but greatly perturbed. Now, for interior thought. Some Christly consolation, or metaphysical.

What a radiant sunset! Chilly, however. A brisk walk through the woods. Lights, a town ahead. Some worldly sem-blance, at least.

Carrying the fishing rod. Looking silly. Car-less. Soon wife-less. Probably jobless, too.

Things will look up. He's out of the lake, that too-small boat.

He's very cold. He's directed to the police by a staring stranger.

No sympathy from the police. He'll wait out the night at a rough inn, then look in to the police station tomorrow for news of the car, having given them a description to keep them busy with, as they hunt down "clues."

If the car doesn't materialize, he'll leave his phone number and address and take the train homeward in the morning.

Great to get back home again. Nothing like it. After today.

Home is where his heart lay. A new job, a new wife, in a new future.

Thus, his life lay ahead. A vision, bred of bad times.

To transcend these bad times. Having survived them, there'd be an ideal lake, on a warm day. Fish being caught. Hot sweat. Joy. Freedom. Lazy zest. Ease of life. Not a speck, on the home horizon—all in order, there.

Later. Till such a day, let there be endurance for now. Sorely tried.

Sorely dealt with. Fate took a wrong turning, here.

His infancy hardly prepared him for *this*.

For he was fully grown. Within his hope, be stretched to his full groan.

LXXIII. FISHING, FALLING IN, DRYING OFF. AN AL-LEGORY AT THE EDGE OF LIFE'S LAKE.

Al Lehman went fishing but fell in. Luckily he was wearing his waterproof boots, or he would have caught his death of a cold leading to such complications as, at least, pneumonia. As it was, he did get wet, but only from head to knees rather than from head to feet. The getting wet included such upper extremities as his arms themselves, up to and including such appendages as his fingers down to the very tips, getting thereby both hands wet, not to mention chest, stomach, the notorious buttock-pelvis area (the seat of many moral controversies), the upper legs stopping at the knees where his tight waterproof boots were securely fastened at the top, preventing his feet from getting wet (or at least moist), which would have led to pneumonia or at least the sniffles.

His neck and head got doused, too, as well as shoulders and down, but not further down than the knees.

The fish had a good laugh at his expense. There he was, trying to fool them to their very destruction, lure them under false pretenses of giving them a free meal; but *they* have the last laugh on *him*.

Serves him right, to have fallen in. But the lake is shallow there, so he scrambles back up to the bank or shore, shaking water off himself like a shaggy dog.

Did he lose his fishing rod? No, there it is, dangling half in, half out, with the worm bait having meanwhile been made a cautious meal of by fish who knew how to avoid the fatal hook, their metallic invitation to danger.

Al Lehman has regained his poise. He dries himself off in a near-by sunny patch. He's ready to try again, undaunted by humiliation at the hands (hands?) of fish: not that they (the fish) were responsible for his falling in—not directly so, but they *were* the cause of his fishing there in anyway the first place; which if he hadn't been doing, he'd not have been near enough to the lake for his misadventure to take place in the form of a splash, replacing momentarily a perturbed oval area at the edge of the body of tranquil surface water under which the fish held their neat traffic levels in gliding darts and skimming non-collisions.

He tosses in, once more, the fly of hooked bait, lining out a wide arc from the practised rod. He remains dry, wades in with his guardian rubber boots, and gets a few catches, which he collects in a tight net to bring back home to civilization in his car at the afternoon's end: which it is now; so he's driving back, dry and calm. Nearing the city, he's stalled in a traffic jam. Finally he gets back, but late. Marge is asleep. Things aren't well between them. He wants to separate, but she's pregnant. He'll be a father, but must remain with a woman he no longer loves.

He puts the fish in the refrigerator and cooks his own dinner from other food from there. Marge wakes up, surly, petulant, peevish, disheveled, and shares the food. She mocks the size and number of the fish he caught today. She'd mock and knock at whatever pretext, for she's down on him. Their unborn child is their reluctant bond.

Al accepts this now; or puts up with it; for he must. Being a father is a privilege to be paid for. His job is also turning out badly: hanging over him is the likelihood of dismissal. The times are hard for replacing the job. He's fishing in the lake of life, but falls in though his boots keep the lower legs dry. He's on his last dry legs. The fish are few to be caught, and meager.

A bad spell.

The world is a lake's edge. He's not doing well. But wait. It won't always be this way. He'll divorce Marge when the child is out of infancy. He'll get a good new job he likes. He'll catch a splendid girl, in the lake of romance, falling in for her, getting wet, but hooking her. Life's lake will yield better. Thus he angles. Pauses and rests. In his dry spell. Grown content, on hope's tall tale. Biding his narrow time. On troubled waters, waiting it all out. For waiting's his only game. With the meager catch he has. Toward the promised tug, on the truer lake.

LXXIV. THE CAT PAT'S NON-MORTALITY-AWARENESS

Al Lehman was aware that his cat Pat, who was old as cats go by the scale of cats' average longevity duration ratio, was doomed some day to die.

His awareness of his cat Pat's mortality was made more poignant by the fat fact that the cat Pat himself was limited (due to the species he belonged to) to no awareness himself that he would some day die.

So Al Lehman had to be aware for both of them of their double impending deaths.

He looked at his cat Pat. Poor little thing. It had an Irish human name (anything Irish is human, except for the vegetable, mineral, and animal kingdoms in Ireland that simply aren't).

Poor little cat Pat. Al Lehman had their deaths down pat. First it would be Pat's turn, then, long years afterward, his own.

He knew that his wife Marge, from whom he was estranged and soon to be divorced, knew well enough about her own mortality to exempt Al from having to be aware or it *for* her, as he was for his cat Pat.

Their son Gregory, who was residing with Marge, was by now old enough to be more than dimly aware of his own awful impending mortality years and years hence—presumably quite a while after his parents have shuffled off to meet their separate fates.

Al's mother and foster-father were closer to that "divine" date, and surely their awareness would be brimming with it.

Al's father had no awareness at all of anything by now, being completely "in the grave," as the saying goes.

Al's two brothers and their respective wives—four more separate sets of awareness.

But cat Pat—cute little thing—is sweetly oblivious, the little brute.

Al Lehman plays with him, then gets bored, since cat Pat can offer only limited fun, belonging to such a limited species with dim awareness, of the present only.

Al Lehman is tired of cat Pat. This is Saturday. No work at the office today. Al Lehman is home in the apartment. Tonight he has a date with a potentially exciting new girl whom he met at a party last week.

He can imagine all he wants about her, since he's had no experience of her beyond talking with her at last week's crowded party on a few scattered occasions near clusters of people. He can dream into how he might imagine her to be. He's to call on her with his car and take her to a restaurant. Now, he's playing with his limited cat Pat. Whose death is known by the human Al, but not by its little four-legged subject, who lives only for the present—if for that.

Tonight will be romantic or erotic maybe. Spiked by mortality's fine flavor, heightened by mortality's acid herb.

Cat Pat goes to sleep on a chair, curled up into a fur-ball. Al Lehman goes to sleep on his bed, stretched out. That's his momentary cure for boredom. Tonight is excitement, potentially ahead. A girl he doesn't know, but has hopes for. Romantic, erotic, glorious spice. Heady, enticing. Boredom-killers. Mortality-delayers. Prime distractions, high awareness packed deep. Close human company. Close and tight. Hugs, and ecstasy.

He's asleep, in the late afternoon. He'll wake up refreshed. He'll ignore cat Pat, save to feed him.

He's all fired up. The date is soon.

Who is she? Death's matchless rival, tonight.

LXXV. THE GLOBAL PLAGUE OF OUR SORROW

Unaccountably, Al Lehman was feeling so sad that his sadness scared his friends away for fear of social contagion to such an epidemic degree that the plague could be catching and they'd come down with the misery bug.

All but one friend kept distance to isolate and quarantine the carrier of the dread disease. The exception was Harry, but why? He was now immune, having been inoculated with a stiff injection of a bout of recent melancholy depression. Thus he'd paid his dues, and was free to unavoid Al Lehman, unlike the others, who took a leave of absence from their dangerously infected friend.

Harry played a cheerful role while Al Lehman brooded. "You're only *temporarily* sad," chirped the merry Harry.

But Al Lehman continued sinking. Harry's jolly compassion of mirth was brushed dead aside.

Then Harry turned to logic. "What *causes* such determined unhappiness?" he asked, galvanizing Al Lehman's faculties for explanation, truth, clarity, and expression, previously in the dormant state, quiescently glazed in a cake of melancholy ice.

"I'm alive such a short time. I missed all the historical ages for centuries before. And I'll miss all the later ones following my lifetime. I miss out on so much: not just eras and epochs, but places too, in which they all happen. I'm present only to a few local events. They chain together, unevenly, to form my little knot of experience. Others have *their* lives. My own is bound in, and finite. It's rounded off, in a humble duration of observed life. That's all I get, personally. It's my only lot. Isn't that depressing? *Now* cheer me up, Harry."

But Harry was miserable. He had been inoculated immune, but came down with the sadness virus again. A cosmic brand of it. Mortality's moan, within the historic immortality—comparatively speaking—of that glorious infinity unknown to any individual, known only to the race as a whole, in lumpen collectivity, pieced together from individual segments, from fitful fragments of separate lives, endured apart, roughly connected to the abstract racial totality of our kind, the slow human organism that fashions all of time from lost brief cells, like Al Lehman's.

LXXVI. Caught between adultery and fidelity; mating them; with strange issue.

Al Lehman was about to be unfaithful to his wife whom he loved. The "other woman" had made it unmistakably clear that her invitation to her apartment this evening was not for a tame chat, but rather for the solemn seriousness of sincere pleasure, the profound business of honest—painfully honest—, close, direct, deep communication, baring their souls and breasts to each other. How frighteningly earnest!

But he loved Marge, the woman he married, pregnant with his own child.

He was betraying her! Adultery at last! Complete and unadulterated. He was an adult.

No longer a young groom, a hardworking, devoted husband.

He was about to despoil the family nest.

From wife Marge, to "girlfriend" Charlotte. A study in contrast?

No! They were as alike as twins, in all essential respects!

In that case, what had Charlotte to offer that he didn't get at home from dear Marge?

Illicit excitement. Tightroping along the abyss of the forbidden.

The intrigue of the clandestine!

The thing was: Marge should never find out! The diplomatic discretion of the master spy, supreme in the crafts of secrecy, in the witchcraft of occult mystification, cloaked in vast obscurity, was the role Al Lehman must carefully practice, if he were to get the best of two worlds, and eat while having his cake of forbidden fruit.

To carry on an affair while being a thoroughly married family man preparing to welcome a presumed son to worldly travail, would take duplicity, deception, and wile.

But it would be worth-wile to pursue such mutually incompatible ends as remaining a model husband while enjoying a nice steady piece on the side.

Why, you old rascal! The devil himself, in his immaculately virtuous pose.

Not so much immaculate virtue, as immaculate pose.

Well, he could carry it off! Was he not a man of parts: part husband, and part "lover"?

All adding up to a lively whole! A most finished whole!

Self-congratulations took over; while guilt and self-doubt, remorse and misgiving, fell complacently into place.

You old devil! So is that you, Al Lehman? You slick adventurer!

From the office he's directly visiting Charlotte, having furnished the "working-very-late-at-the-office-tonight" excuse, to a trusting wife. "Don't worry about me, Marge. It's an emergency session, with extra clients and their extra accounts. Don't wait up, go to sleep. The staff might be given nearby hotel rooms tonight. Tomorrow morning's deadline *must* be met—no 'if' or 'but.' Else, we're all out of a job."

Marge understood. And it might mean a raise. A promotion. Security, with their child coming.

Marge was proud to be so understanding. Al was proud to put one over on her.

She was putty, under his dissembling thumb. Deceiving her was like stealing candy from a raw babe's fist.

Five-thirty, work was done. Now to become a man's man, a two-timer, with flair and wicked grace.

His groin throbbed. A bulging pulse. A rising surge of gay abandon.

※

He was on his way. To his moral doom, on the subway.

Out of the destined station, the walk to the fatal building. Fidelity's formal execution.

The ring at the doorbell. Door opened. By Charlotte. Seduction's threshold. Sin, by the traditional method.

She leads him in, takes his coat, offers a drink, after telling him where to sit. He's in her control.

He's excited. He's breathless. Nervous, with concealed panic.

Charlotte is dressed to slay the fully armed heart. Her skirt reveals as it conceals. Al is mutely staring, from his soft chair, sitting far back, grown docile, in captive passivity. He'll be seduced. In subdued obedience. Girlish, female. Charmed to a titter, by the bold rush of Charlotte: Charlotte, a real man. Exchanging sexes, for this reversible occasion.

He's forced to spend the night with her. Marge had been prepared to expect no phone call, in an overnight business emergency.

"You're too dominating," complained Charlotte's lover, lying side by side in bed before sleep.

He felt guilt toward Marge, who—he hoped not—might prematurely have her labor tonight.

An adulterer!

A clean kid! Transformed to a dirty husband.

He's asleep. A stranger in someone's bed.

He dreams he's in his own bed. Or rather, inside Marge, for he's the one she's pregnant with. He's due for birth.

From womb to world. He's coiled inside, ready. Marge screams, and the doctor delivers him from her.

He's safe, outside. His own son. Conveyed by his own wife. Swept through, into this new world.

LXXVII. A JOB WE CAN'T KNOW ABOUT

After his separation and divorce, and with the nation in an economic recession, and with alimony and child-support to spend, Al Lehman had the panic to be caught in the worst possible state: between jobs.

He urgently followed up the diminishing want ads, and filled out resumés and curriculum vitaes at various employment agencies; leading in a few cases to interviews by personnel directors of firms that retained sufficient vitality to be actually hiring in those hard times.

He was so desperate as to accept an odd offer that ordinarily he would at least have hesitated over. It led him into strange things, into rare dimensions, other spheres, on totally different planes. The realm of experience he was brought to by his new position has no equivalence by any normal approximate level; and so, not even by metaphor's aid, or allegory's broad method, can language bring expression and communication, much less reporting, to what uniquely Al Lehman underwent, in the course of that job he took.

But now it's over. He's back here, among his kind, with common points of reference to the framework of human unification.

What was that job like? What did it entail? With what, thereby, was he in contact? Can he talk about it?

No. It's an information blank, void, or gap, in what otherwise is his life's social continuum.

Factually, then, the record on Al lehman is now permanently incomplete, lacking any truth indication as to that strange job he took. For those outside himself, it constitutes an ongoing wonder, the pure mystery of the unknown. For *himself,* what does it mean, that period in his life when he had that job? He's not revealing it. How can *we* tell, if *he* won't?

Then speculation and conjecture get to work, hypotheses, guesses, rumors, and all those other substitutes for information. Word is getting around. It's circulating. To no, though, direct effect. Al Lehman won't confirm or deny anything. On that subject, he maintains strict muteness, as its only source, the true bona fide authority whose testimony can at all convince or count.

The curtain is down, and remains down, on that short act in his life. (It was only a short time, yes, we know *that* much.)

The context of before and after that act leads to nothing definite. Let's cut short this disappointment, and not even inquire any more. We'll simply drop our interest and betray not the slightest curiosity.

Even that, however, won't make him talk. Let, then, that stone silence of his be the very last word, the definitive comment, consumation, and summary, on what's his. We know nothing of the what of it, so it can't be ours. As such, we depart from his life, but join it at other points, which he makes accessible, in the shared lot of all our experience, the common pool where whatever happened to an individual enriches collective fact in the human myth.

LXXVIII. RUTH POURS HOT LOVE OVER AL LEHMAN. YET, IN THE END, WHO BURNS?

After his divorce, with wife Marge and son Gregory off his hands after years of love and tension, Al Lehman felt a free surge of release, a gay buoyant abandon that commemorated the end of long strain. He went on a "girl-a-week" binge, with irresponsible promiscuity. For the most part, the girls enjoyed it, playing along with the temporariness of these games.

However, there was one moody exception: Ruth, who felt such a possessive passion for Al Lehman that she wouldn't let him go, spied on her rivals, her possible successors and those whom she succeeded, and insanely brooded even murder (of Al Lehman, not any of her rivals), when the rage of jealousy gripped her in demonic frenzy.

Al Lehman tactfully tried to get rid of her, but she held on and wouldn't let go. She demanded total marriage, his abdication of all freedom, his devotion to her for the remainder of his life.

She brought brutal coercion to bear, using emotional blackmail or any other tactical weapon at hand. Al Lehman's honor was his vulnerable point, which she exploited fully, in the pure destruction that only love can breed.

Al Lehman carefully resisted. How grave and delicate, to feel revulsion and yet not dare to reject.

Her desperation was precariously close to homicide. She was too love-maddened to scruple. Here was a new untenable bondage for Al Lehman, to rival the bitter last phases of marriage to Marge prior to final breakup.

He abandoned his girl-a-week binge, of necessity, submitting to Ruth's ruthless curtailment of his freedom. He was her prisoner. She forced him to give up his own cosy carefree bachelor apartment, to move in with her and do her bidding. He had to move his collections and possessions to his mother's basement, for indefinite storage.

He contemplated running away out of town, but he had an important job essential to a promising career; leaving it would amount virtually to professional suicide. So he had "no choice," but to stay.

Perhaps he could get Ruth committed to a mental institution. Hers was a pathological possessiveness, and her jealousy knew only murder for its definite limit.

But how could he actually *prove* her insanity, to the institutional authorities? It might backfire, and she'd punish him, by tightening the clamps and reinforcing shackles. Then he'd have to despair for even minimal liberties, while her rule would toughen tyrannical and hem him in.

"Ruth, you persecute me with your obsession for me. You must fall out of love, or you'd destroy me. I'll perish, the way things are going."

"No, Al. I'll force you to base a new flourishing upon my despotic reign."

"But Ruth, I simply don't love you; nor will I ever. Have you no pride? Relinquish me, or you crush us both."

"You'll *grow* to love me, in time. I'm determined to that, and will bend *your* own will to it, too."

"I'll revolt, before that. I'll overthrow you, and violently."

"You already have, my dear: I'm your servile love, forever."

How could he get out of it? His doom was sealed: or so it seemed, as the prison walls clanked, with steely might.

He's stuck. What will save him? Perhaps the reader can offer suggestions. Mail them to Al Lehman, care of Hell Itself.

However, all letters are burned, automatically, upon delivery to that torrid zone.

Same with telegrams. So don't write; phone. Use the direct hot line. He'll answer, with his scalding voice. He'll begin: "Rescue me," then he'll listen. But Ruth is monitoring the phone conversation. Just before you can get to the point, she'll go "click" on you: you're cut off.

If *you* are, Al Lehman is more so. He's devoured, but slowly, while living, enveloped, immersed, in flames of love.

Ruth is on fire, for him? *He*'s on fire. She cooly fans the blaze. Yet he'll never perish. Honor is his asbestos suit. He sweats and melts, under it. But bears up, under all that heat.

But it wilts Ruth, who doles it out and burns. *She*'s consumed. She'd played with fire. Al Lehman survives. Charred and singed. He celebrates his freedom with a North Pole vacation. And coldly reflects, on his long captivity.

LXXIX. FIDELITY IN ABUNDANCE

Al Lehman thought back: "All the women known. Through the last thirty years. Different times, different phases. Different feelings, different women. Now, they're all mixed together, assembled from eighty-five bodies, mingled from eighty-five faces, all flowered into one montage, the composite of separate hours and separate places.

"All dumped into my one small cell of imagery, clustered finer in cluttered mutual replacings. Collectively represented in their singular multiple.

"A thirty years' unity by me. One of me to each of them, and all of me to every one.

"I was abundantly faithful. To the whole lot, I stood steadfast in my constancy.

"Thirty years gave me a fickle appearance.

"But I was *true*—one by one.

"And the truth spread thin."

LXXX. LEVELS OF REMAINING DISCONNECTED

Impotence and frigidity are mutually cooperative—but toward the negative, alas.

Al Lehman found himself impotent with a girl who coincidentally discovered herself to be frigid in their simultaneous first attempt at some mating arrangement. Their double inhibition hardly generated a successful union. On the contrary, their debacle was jointly humiliating.

They failed to make ends meet. Their meat pursued vain ends, meeting, at the end, with the joint result of an adjourned joining.

"Two wrongs don't make a right," they verbally agreed, to couple with their physical agreement to uncouple themselves apart in opposition to their thwarted wish for dear oneness as the agreeable concord longed for in their separate dissatisfactions.

They tried again, but remained disconnected.

Frustration yielded to futility. They were resigned to renounce even trying; for trying had been too trying, in both their cases.

"Let's be only friends," Al Lehman platonically suggested, but amended, "as though we had a choice."

She sadly agreed. But they had nothing further in common. They were even incompatible as friends.

They spoke from different mental languages.

They gave up that abortive attempt at friendship, to part forever. This parting provided a basis for a strangely negative unity.

LXXXI. THE LONELIEST SUBJECT: WOMEN

"Women are so sexually appealing," Al Lehman concluded, after years of specializing in that subject, conducting private in-
vestigations and a wealth of personal research that qualified
him as a self-styled or self-professed expert in that vividly incomplete science. Women! Why, volumes of books alone could
well be written on such an endless subject! He sighed. The sigh
was wordlessly expressive: bespeaking whole volumes, sequel
by sequel, that could barely cover even the minor inconsisten-
cies of that unlimited field. Once more, he sighed. Words failed,
or fled, at the impossibility of conveying even the slightest introductory sketch, the barest approach, to that female branch
of the human species.

What more was there to say, beyond the eloquence of that
mere nothing?

He was speechless. Women! The concept itself was hope-
lessly staggering, under its own unbearable burden. It was pal-
pably intangible, yet concretely abstract. It gushed with mystery. Experience nibbled at its knowledge. The romance of dra-
matic sentiment veiled it. Such lame words as "love" and "lust"
feebly limped along, in the parody of a paralleling. They indicated nought. They couldn't signify. The subject entirely eluded
them.

When Al Lehman, though, married Marge, he became
disillusioned. She was finite. One woman. Confounding all
"women."

Women in the absolute? What were they? Al Lehman's problem was a particular one: Marge; as he was hers. Banality re-
placed mystery. Romance disintegrated. It couldn't be held up.
The union cracked. Divorce. Their son Gregory went with the

mother. "Women" no longer fascinated Al Lehman. A long convalescence set in. He's cautious, now. He doesn't veil his eyes. He must take a hard look. He must open bold defenses, cynically buttressed up by bitterness. Women? The subject was loaded with harm. He learned skills of deception. He took a cold guard, from that warm regard. He divided women into this woman, and that. He broke down their incomprehensible vastness. He atomized them. In predatory caginess, to prey upon such cunning snares, with the hunter's guile.

Women? This one and that. Take measured steps. Keep a cautious tread. They were his magnificent enemies. Such scented glow, such subtle dazzle! His resistance melted. Mutely, he could only adore. He blurred all soft, to their round ooze.

LXXXII. WINNING ALL THE WOMEN'S HEARTS AT ONE PARTY. THERE WAS NO COMPETITION —SAVE *FOR* HIM. IT WAS ALL TOO COMPLETE.

Finding himself, by strange wonder, at a party where hordes of available, unescorted girls were left alluringly unbalanced by any corresponding number of male possible counterparts, Al Lehman was in a competitive situation but was virtually uncompeted with. He seemed miraculously in possession of a whole field of ripe glamor that cried out "pluck me," in lonely tones of easy female accessibility, promising love's lifetime from sexual immediacy. Was he only dreaming? No, this was solidly being true. It was real, by actual experience in the world. And here was the world, at this party. Of greater promise than dazzling dream's delusion.

The competitive situation he was in, in which he himself was virtually uncompeted with, found him being the one competed *for*.

This was an enviable position to be in. He was on a ride up to the high ego clouds of pride.

To maintain this stunning romantic advantage, this princely privilege as the mystery favorite whose favors were highly being bidden for in a market woven cunningly in speculation richly decked out in the arts of seduction and intrigue, enchantment, enticing glories of chance-encountered amours, the wicked spontaneity of impulsive choice, naughty whimsy glazed over humbly in radiant protection from the sober grimness of deliberation's chill primness, Al Lehman prudently refrained from favoring any girl over the others; withheld any indication of preference; this kept the competition glowing, and exalted his rare, exquisite masculine value to a majestic remoteness, the supreme "catch," the most improbable of snares, just beyond each lovely girl's frantic strain of reach, with her deliciously contoured, flowing arm extended to the tip itself of each finger's utmost stretch.

He kept them all dangling, perched in the precarious pessimism of suspense and despair. Hope was denied from none. Each spun waves of allure at him, to which he managed never quite yet to succumb.

The few other men, who could have been possible rivals, abandoned the contest, leaving the entire party field of bountiful women to that armor-clad knight on a high steed, emblems blazing, the tournament's banner-proclaiming hero, the sole lord of the fray strewn with imploring, writhing captive women, each a plunderable bundle of wild round willingness, softly aflame for Al Lehman, whose noble might and main strode through profuse beauty's garden of overblown blooms.

He carefully ignored and disdained his suitresses, while yet catching each one intimately by the eye in private side encouragement. These contradictory signals from him brought neurotic frenzy to those would-be brides bulging with scarcely covert proposals to be abducted and ravished by the passionately permitted, adorably entreated Al Lehman, who subdued their total hearts to vows of breathless obedience, submissive panting for the least bone of love he'd toss in the careless squander of his majestic hoard to kneeling suppliants for what they dare to covet without meriting, in dire deprived desperation and anguished longing's audacious terror.

But in keeping *all* on the string, as the party wore on and the hour grew terribly late, there was the danger that Al Lehman would wind up, in fact, in final conclusion, with none whatever of these so many willing women.

He gave the nod to none and played no favorite. Then each and all gave up and went trooping home, in a mass, in one consensus of defeat, in scattered directions diversely to solitary beds.

All from the same party door. Inside, Al Lehman lingered yet briefly.

Nothing to show for this evening of his eminence. Such lonely termination, of such prodigious promise. Profusely adored in plenty, his immodesty had risen above choice. With such choice opportunity, he chose not to choose. The "too-much" became all-or-nothing. Paralyzed by the all, he couldn't cope or manage to select, weed out, eliminate, decide upon. He possessed the total all, but only temporarily. From there, the fall to nothing stood complete.

Empty-handed, empty-armed. No trophies, from that rare dream-party of sweeping triumph, of conquest so complete that nothing was left over for any further lesser day. The night sufficed, that party. Then all gain vanished, as the equation burned itself out in self-repletion, with no remainder to humbly testify, as to that brilliant night.

LXXXIII. AL LEHMAN'S SUCCESSION OF LOVES. THERE'S NO DISCERNIBLE PATTERN, IN THAT SUCCESSION. AND IT GOES ON, THIS SUCCESSION. A NEW ONE GAINED, FOR THAT ONE LOST.

"I've been the object of women's reformation or reclamation projects," brooded Al Lehman, reminiscing in solitude on the women he had known and their various intentions to remold him, remake him, remodel him, by partial aspect or thorough essence, according to their diverse schemes, tastes, claims, and interests for colonizing his traits, co-opting his character as malleable subject for imperialistic manipulation, grafting on his faculties the patterns specified to his assorted feminine subjections.

He'd snap back into place, and none of it worked. They haven't done a thing to modify him.

Yes they have. He's adjusted to them. He's had to, in order to have them.

Each one he had, he was with for a longer or shorter time, then broke up with. Then the next one, and so forth. Each meant a new adjustment. He was pliant. He had to be. Then, he'd snap back into place.

As what?

As himself, for the next one.

And so on. So many selves. So many women. They all had so many plans for him. With each, he went along—for a while.

When will he really settle down? He did, with marriage to Marge, and some long affairs after their breakup.

What is he? To each woman, he's what she wants him to be, up to the critical point.

What *is* that critical point? When one affair has gone its limit, and snaps? When the next one is ripe for birth, to his exchanging extent?

They'd wish they'd only know. They've lost him, and some gladly.

He's obedient to his current one. She's building vast plans.

LXXXIV. THE FOUR LOVES OF THREE PEOPLE, WHO STRUGGLE TO SQUARE THE ODDS EVEN AND MATCH OUT MAGICALLY THE DISJOINTED TRIANGLE, TO WRENCH SOMEHOW A UNITY FROM THEIR JOINT AND JANGLING DISCORD.

Al Lehman had a severe problem: two women were in love with him, both of whom he also was in love with. Ideally and abstractly, the most direct solution would be the mathematical magic of an identical second Al Lehman sprouting in miraculous full-formed duplication from the first. That would take care of the second of the two women, both of whom he loved and who loved him.

However, no identical second Al Lehman ever came about. There remained only the one and original, which now became a limitation rather than a sufficiency, in view of the harsh problem of two women and two requited loves, both of them urgent and compelling, each as serious and solemn in its own right as any unique fatal passion in the all-or-never doom of once-in-a-lifetime romantic totality.

Is a problem really a problem if it's insoluble?

Hester Miller and Stephanie Ferris were the two women in "question." To counterbalance them, there was merely only one Al Lehman, all by himself. The equation didn't come out foursquare. Tragic heartbreak would have to fill the remainder.

Sometimes Hester Miller seemed *the* one for him; other times Stephanie Ferris was *the* only one. Such vacillation, pendulum-like, in click-clock alternation, couldn't be kept perpetually up mechanically. A *choice* must be made. Yes, ultimately, he must choose. But "choose" is an ugly word, in these two cases. For he must lose and relinquish one, by dreadful, half-destructive choice.

He would die, rather than lose and relinquish one. Thus, the insoluble problem took on proportions of grotesque morbidity, of wretched horror, even of a crime against the natural radiance of spiritual harmony. Fair, sweet love, grown foul in its own asymmetry.

Love is so important, that who would forgo it? But when it doubles itself simultaneously, its importance is unhandable. The coping stops. Reality slides away. Monsters are born, from instability.

A top-level conference must be held, among the principals involved. Not all four, alas, but all three—the imponderable number three—would be summoned to the crucial meeting. What would be item number one on the agenda to be discussed? Perhaps vital decisions would be rendered. Or, a mere stalemate could result. The possibilities were open, and not neatly to be numbered.

Stephanie Ferris arrived first, to Al Lehman's apartment, at the appointed hour, followed shortly thereafter by her one and only rival, Hester Miller. Now, the showdown was imminent.

Al Lehman, by joint consent, was the moderator, master of ceremonies, arbitrator, conductor, of this key conference. That seemed only fair, in view of those peculiar circumstances.

Hester and Stephanie were not uncomfortable with each other. They spoke calmly, respectfully, without evident rivalry, malice, sarcasm, distrust, or bad will.

The proceedings were orderly. It was all on a civilized basis. But for practical purposes, no headway toward conclusion of any actual consequence seemed likely to be made. What did the polite, steady decorum matter? What though all was on a civil footing? The insoluble remained as such. "No way out." The likelihood of the intolerable status quo was unchallenged. Nothing drastic was counterpoised, in radical alternative. The mold was hardened, on this solidly triangular impasse of love unlucky in its odd number. Where could the evening-up be found? Three wouldn't fit, here, into anything basically sound.

"Well, Hester and Stephanie, we've conferred a long time, but to no avail. All suggestions have been considered, but none has power to shake this immovable problem from its fundamentally unshakable foundations of dreary insolubility.

"In view of this, let's adjourn our meeting but appoint another session at which time, perhaps, a new light will be shed, however futile that prospect must seem from the viewpoint of tonight's failure. I can't ask one of you to remain and sleep with me, at this moment, for it would be unfair to the other, in our delicate predicament of awkward triangularity, in which common frustration we're joint stockholders, although the share of you two in it must of course exceed mine by misery's degree, or else in some way differ, for each of you has only one of me, whereas both of you are mine, in my great cross between good and bad fortune."

"When shall our next conference be held?" Hester or Stephanie then asked. A date was agreed upon, and the two women kissed Al Lehman goodbye, leaving together at the same time. They took the same subway. One got off at an earlier stop, the other at a later station. Each went home to sleep alone; as did Al Lehman, remaining where he was. A common night bound all three, in separate solitudes. A trio of lonely sleepers. Each thinking of the other two.

The night was endless. Three sets of endless dreams. Three eternal nights. Eternity, divided by three. Or multiplied eternity, stuck frozen in that knotted bond.

Forever. Till the next morning.

Al Lehman woke up with his choice. The definite choice. Hester Miller? Stephanie Ferris? Who?

Neither. To perpetuate the trinity, to immortalize it, he rejected them both, as the pair, the same pair they were when he loved them both. That way, all three remained "inseparable." As a spiritual unity.

There was another meeting planned. Should he tell them both his decision then? Or not wait, but tell them separately, by phone?

His "heart" was broken, in two places. Stephanie's heart would be broken only in one; Hester's, only in one.

Four heartbreaks. Three people. Love's divinity, damned infernally by some clumsy arithmetic. And in that lump sum, left forever.

LXXXV. AL LEHMAN WAS SO TIRED, BUT THE PARTY WASN'T OVER YET. THE HOSTESS OFFERED HIM HER BED, BUT THE GUESTS HADN'T LEFT. MEANWHILE, WHAT HAPPENED TO AL LEHMAN'S TIREDNESS, AND TO AL LEHMAN HIMSELF? AS WELL AS THE LINGERING GUESTS, AND, OF COURSE, THE HOSTESS?

I was so tired, I couldn't even yawn.

How did you express your tiredness, in that case?

By *looking* tired.

Did it work?

Everybody caught on at once. One even offered a bed.

On the spot?

It happened to be in her apartment, just a few inches away from the offered bed, which was handy and convenient, at the time, considering my utter state of exhaustion which created an instant appearance of tiredness, for all to see, especially the one who offered her bed's immediate hospitality, as soon as her other guests (of whom I was one) should leave, leaving, as it were, the coast clear, for me to jump on the bed and relax.

But that would be a long wait, till the other guests would be cleared out, as the party slowly dawdled interminably toward its delayed conclusion with lingering sociability. How, Al Lehman, were you able to wait?

My tiredness was too exhausted by fatigue to long endure.

What took its place?

Vivacity, animation, excitement, sparkle, energy. It wore the others out, and they fled, leaving only my hostess and myself, alone, together, at last.

Well, it was worth waiting for; not that you *passively* waited, Al Lehman, but rather hastened the event, by influencing the undesirably remaining guests to leave before otherwise they would have gotten around to it. Once the door was closed on the last of them, Al Lehman, leaving your hostess and you together alone, was your previous tiredness restored to you in a later version, so that the opportunity of a bed right nearby for instant sleep satisfaction should have the ripe application of your advantage?

No. I was even wider awake than before. I looked in vain for that lost tiredness. Under cover, it had fled.

How under cover, when you weren't in bed yet?

It just gave me the slip. I thought of chasing my tiredness, but how can you get a hold of a vanished thing?

Only by concept.

Yes, I could *conceive* the tiredness, but not firmly grasp its tangibility, as something felt by the experience of now. I merely remembered it. It was past, and future. Meanwhile, there was my hostess.

The scene is set. You, Al Lehman, are the only remaining guest of a party that's just ended, having started around nine and now it's after midnight, in the weary early hours of the next morning. Your hostess bade you stay when you were tired. Now your tiredness has fled, but still, *you* stay. Has she only one bed?

Yes, but wide enough for both of us.

And you're wide enough awake.

And she's wide enough open, to receive me.

Well, what happened *then*?

I got tired, eventually.

Well, all good things eventually must come to an end.

That's how *I* feel, too. It's a sweet little law, of the universe.

LXXXVI. NATURE-SURPASSING TRUTH

Al Lehman was out hunting on a beautiful Fall day. He had his gun all ready for the advent of some animal to shoot, but also he was taking in what a gorgeous day this was under God's reign. The light was scattered all over the forest through clouds and leaves. The golden orb was lovely in the brisk blue, and floating flecks of white, while fluttering foliage were gaily decked out in early decay.

The ground sloped variously between hilltop ranges and long shades of valley, while Al Lehman trod the middle ground, in hunter's boots, in a bright red jacket that would warn off potential other hunters from using him for a target, for he was wearing human clothes and walking upright, unlike the legitimate specimens of a hunter's righteous prey.

The evergreen trees swayed, the other types swayed, as though in adoration, in love, in longing for eternal blessing. Gleams shone from distant lakes and a sweet waterfall's near-by melody. It was all too lovely. Birds twittered, everywhere. Nature was alive. Its cycle had turned to a beautiful phase. Was it right for Al Lehman to kill? Yes, animals, not people. Nature would approve.

This beauty became a burden. It was too abundant, and was unbearable. Al Lehman was overwhelmed. He yearned to *do* something—like kill.

A crackle through the leaves. There it was, a deer, in the clearing. The sun caught it squarely, as though aiding rifle focus.

Al Lehman made good, with the kill. A clean shot. Dead at once.

Blood over the bright fur. Autumn meant dying. The trees brought in their grave harmony, their flecks of gay decay.

Death's season. Life floated in the lovely light. The deep sun flashed.

Al Lehman never felt happier. He and nature were a tight pair. The woods seemed God-possessed. Some blessing had come down. Catching one dead deer, and live Al Lehman, and the woods around, all in one arresting stroke. Some rare unity, that seemed beyond nature, to which death and life were given minor parts. Mystery struck its slant. And stayed.

LXXXVII. DIVINE WOODLAND LIGHT, ON A SOLITARY HUNTER IN THE HAPPY LENGTH OF HIS DAY.

Armed with a rifle, Al Lehman hunted bear. It was now legal open hunting season.

A divine light was bathing the woods. It came dancing between the trees, it rose from strewn dank leaves on the holy burial ground of dark woodland. It skimmed over the tops of trees, skirting trunks and limbs, illuminating hardy clusters of wildly clinging leaves.

A glow of subdued sparkle brooded sweetly over the entire scene. If light was equated to happiness, was muted light less happy than intense light?

Al Lehman thought this over, rifle dangling, lethal hole downward, from a crooked elbow.

He was hours here already. No bear, but deer could be less rare. The baring of deer would dearly make it bearable to find no bear.

A hare bounded along, and other furry rodents.

Birds swooped and bounced on imaginary points of air.

Hours had passed. His silent gun grew heavier with unused shot.

A long Saturday, away from the commercial office, away from wife and son, from the city apartment.

Alone, swarmed over by nature. Light came at him, went through him, from behind, from ahead, drenching his forest hunt in atmosphere and unity.

He was happy, without killing. But his happiness included the likelihood of his killing. It was still only early afternoon. Somewhere, the deer or bear would come.

On sharp points of light, on muted blurs of light, his happiness draped and dangled itself.

This sweet forest.

He unbackpacked himself, took out food and cooking equipment, made a little bonfire in a quiet clearing.

The day was interminable.

Hours were inching along. He expected to kill.

If not bear or deer, then hare or duck.

His food was exquisitely good. He was his own superb cook, on a woodland day where light hovered, or moved like peals of smoke.

In a nearby brook's gurgle, he washed his cooking tools, enjoying the glow of just-after-eating digestion, as his bold torso quaked with rich health.

Hark! His prey! He picked up his gun, poised it in position, and sighted that moving target—hare? bear? duck? deer?

Bang!

Alas, it was a person.

Was a person? Maybe still *is*.

Maybe just a nick. He hurried.

It was another hunter.

An accident. Dead. Al Lehman had faulty eyesight.

No hare or duck, deer or bear, but a man.

Bleeding from the chest. Pulse unmoving. No flicker on the face. Caught calmly in his expression.

Killing was what Al Lehman had intended. Murder was the horror he had done.

The dead man was older than Al.

But not for long. It was as old as the man would ever get. Al had time: he'd catch up.

A ruined day.

The blissful light in the woods. Appetite, with happy killing ahead.

LXXXVIII. KILLING FOR FRIENDSHIP'S SAKE? NO, THAT'S CARRYING DEATH TOO FAR. THERE SHOULD NEVER BE THAT DILEMMA. FRIENDSHIP SHOULDN'T PROPOSE THAT DIRE DEMAND. IT STRAINS ALL LIMITS.

Not enough people were dying; this brought hard tines to undertakers, cemetarians, and funeral parlorians. They applied for financial aid such as subsidies and grants-in-distress, for tiding-over relief while they were all feeling the pinch. Al Lehman undertook to support his local undertaker, during this widespread crisis of a dearth of deaths, by thinking how to provide him with some sorely needed corpses to bury in solemn ceremony and so forth. Filled coffins would mean filled coffers for the needy, deprived undertaker. Murder, however, being illegal and forbidden by law, how was Al Lehman to go about discharging this gentle deed? Yes, how indeed? This was a morbid problem, of sorts. Tommy Bella deserved more business. He had a family to support (a large one, at that), and had been a respectable member of the community ever since Al Lehman first moved in. Further, he and Mrs. Bella were personal family friends of Al Lehman and wife Marge. The four used to play cards together and share other social conventions. Now Tommy Bella needed help—in the form of some good healthy human deaths—for the financial plight he had fallen in. Deaths to pay debts with. Al Lehman had a fine gun collection, as a hunter as well as a collector. Why not as a murderer, too?—for good old Tommy Bella's sake.

But Al Lehman was law-abiding. It's one thing to hunt animals, and kill them, during the forest license season. But to kill one of his own kind?! Such a thought was even inconceivable.

Yes, but Tommy Bella's children weren't eating enough. How he could use a good, timely death now!

The progress of medicine was mainly responsible for Tommy Bella's current woes. Medicine was keeping old people alive who at one time used to die at that age from various physical causes of disease and decay, which now were kept well in check by great strides in the medical profession, which doctors would know about but which the layman considers only magic.

Younger people, down to infancy itself or birth, were also, by medical advances, kept living, who in former times would have tragically untimely deaths and be properly mourned in formal funereal grief undertaken at grim expenses by prosperous undertakers, the Tommy Bellas of their day, in shady unctuous competence and tact, diplomats as they were or ambassadors between the two kingdoms, Life and Death, keeping cordial, amicable relations between the innately combative representatives of those two totally opposite empires.

There was a plague of good health these days; a veritable epidemic of strong, healthy bodies steeled immune to corruption by germinal disease and rotten bacteriological decay that eats away vital life tissues. Organic physical integrity built up biological inviolability, in wholesome self-endurance. Facing these facts of life, how could Tommy Bella feed sufficiently on death? He was well-trained for death, not life. He wanted the dignity of an honest day's work. But cruel medicine is depriving him of that. Medicine is evil, and should be abolished by law! It's injurious, to the undertaker's trade.

Tommy Bella had hit, indeed, on hard times. His family had to switch from meat to bread; from many vegetables to just a few; from exciting salads to dreary ones. He would therefore ask

Al Lehman to do a personal favor. "Al, my funeral establishment is practically moribund, these days. My business is dying, alas. Can you discreetly kill me a few clients, please? If you drum me up a little business, I'll pay you on a commission basis. On, all the mouths I have to feed! Have compassion, and do a good deed."

"But Tommy, though you know I like you, and consider you one of the most decent fellows I've ever known, a sweet, dear, and true friend, I can't commit murder for you! That's what you're asking me to do; you're like Lady Macbeth pleading with Macbeth to kill the Scotch king. I won't take another mortal's blood! I won't!"

"Please don't be so stubborn, Al. I'm a friend in need. Be a friend indeed. Do me this favor, for friendship's sake, please, Al. Just a few deaths, here and there, for which I can be the funeral director. It's merely a business proposition, not a moral one."

"But you just pleaded friendship; now you plead business."

"I'm too distraught, Al, to keep to a consistent line. My wife has to go to the hospital, and one of my children is sick. I submit my case to you as a charity case. We can't scruple when I'm in an emergency. I beg you, to come to my aid with a helping hand, now that I need you. Please, Al. It's a matter of sentiment."

"First on friendship grounds you wildly implore me; then under business stress; now you cite sentiment—akin to friendship, but on broad humanitarian principle. I approve of sentiment to you; you have my rich compassion, my heartfelt sympathy, my profound and personal regrets, for the misfortune currently plaguing you, your honorable wife, and your brood of kids. Yes, but humanitarianism must apply equally to other souls, as well: such as your intended client-victims. Why should *they* suffer?—or rather, their families and friends would suffer, for they would only die. I *want* them to live. I won't kill them. Not even for such a nice guy like you."

"Al, you've turned out to be a disloyal friend. All I'm asking for is some mortal blood of people you don't even know! I can't understand your reluctance."

"I've failed you, Tommy. I've let you down."

"It's unforgivable, Al. I'm not your friend any more. Instead, what I'd like to be is your infernal corpse's embalmer, coffin-quarterer, and burial director. I'll hire a henchmen to do the job on you. Your wife Marge will hire my services, but I won't give her a reduced rate. She'll have to pay, from the bottom of your insurance! Thus, your son Gregory will become too impoverished to go to college. This will be, Al, my subtle revenge on you, for failing me in my crisis. It might sound vindictive to your sensitive ears; but I'm only serving you some just retribution; which, scoundrel that you are, a former friend turned turncoat, you deeply deserve. Death is too good for the likes of you! I'll see you're degraded, by some funeral mishaps; your corpse will be desecrated, perhaps. Marge will weep, and Gregory whine: your slim family shrouded in the gruesome livery of black."

"Tommy, you're too entirely cruel! I forbid you to have my death brought about, for your selfish business interests. My life is important to me. I insist on retaining it—every bit of it."

"You're a selfish pig, Al. You won't even sacrifice your own life, for my just cause."

"Tommy, let our friendship end, on that sour note."

"Agreed, Al. I'll bury you, yet."

They parted company. Forever. Al Lehman, and Tommy Bella. Over a mere life-and-death matter. A terrible little misunderstanding, which they couldn't—or refused to—patch up.

Medicine, the healing progress, was Tommy Bella's true villain. He had to turn to Al Lehman, for compensation in the other direction. In fact, Al Lehman was even going to volunteer it, himself. But then, his own goodness got the better of him: his detestation of killing. In the end, thus, he turned Tommy Bella down. Now, not only medical progress, but Al Lehman too, are Tommy Bella's natural enemies. Life itself is what holds Tommy Bella back, from material prosperity. Yet, he values his own, and those of his family.

Al Lehman likes to keep human life alive in a healthy state—it's only animals that he hunts, as well as of course fish. It's with human beings that he draws the divine line—refusing to harm them. This qualm was what Tommy Bella had found so perverse. With *that* shady character, business always came first.

How had those two been such fast friends? Well, their wives had liked each other, and then those men liked each other too.

Not any more: they're divided—life from death. In principle, in effect.

Let's hope Tommy Bella doesn't try to get Al Lehman killed, for revenge. It would be excessive, that measure. It would stink, of disrespect for life. Of contempt, for another soul.

Al Lehman had the *superior* soul. So far as souls went, Tommy Bella believed in their demise—in full bodily form.

He thrives, on death. Al Lehman is better off, without him.

It's *good* their friendship's over. May Al Lehman never entertain another idea of killing—of depriving human strangers of their lives, to promote the welfare of one already known.

Relieving a friend's distress is fine—but within limits.

The outer limit is death. A sacred boundary, to observe.

LXXXIX. A MORAL CONSULTANT

"Virtue is its own reward, but I'm always on the lookout for a bonus," Al Lehman confided to his moral consultant.

"Naturally," agreed his easy-going moral consultant. "You want what you can get. Within, of course, the acceptable moral limit."

"I'm always after pleasure, that's my primary aim," Al Lehman went on, ignoring his moral consultant's yes-man assurances of unstrict permissibility for most conduct or behavior in the moral sphere's field of action and consequence.

"Delight, bliss, ecstasy, comfort, convenience, advantage, favor, good fortune, satisfaction, nice feelings, gratification, fulfillment, happiness, full flourishing, high thriving, gainful endeavor—that's what I want," Al Lehman listed, for his moral consultant's benefit.

The latter, however, warned Al Lehman not to "step over the line."

"*What* line?" retorted Al Lehman, quick to be ruffled, now offended and waxing indignant. His virtue seemed implicated and open to question, if not sullied by accusation. In fact, it felt thoroughly maligned. He briefly considered firing his moral consultant for a rash deed of insubordination, a breach of faith, and a nasty insinuation. Instead, Al Lehman demanded an explanation.

"Don't harm others. That's what I mean by not stepping over the line. Satisfy yourself, short of that."

Al Lehman accepted this condition, and retained his moral consultant—even increasing his slight salary somewhat, for having established the bounds of requisite goodness to sanctify Al Lehman's selfish pursuits.

The moral consultant still only receives a "nominal" fee—a minor boost over before. But that's all his work *ought* to earn. Al Lehman, now, knows his limits—they're his own limits. He has what he wants—no need to overstep them.

The moral consultant is redundant. But he's there, out of habit. He reports to duty. But doesn't consult. Al Lehman knows what to do, and what not, by himself.

One day, the moral consultant never reported. He didn't even "call in sick."

He's unheard from, yet. Al Lehman goes on, without him. From time to time, he inquires what ever became of his old moral consultant. But no-one else can inform him. The moral consultant seems to have vanished.

He was *such* a nice man.

So nice, he's not even needed.

His loss isn't even missed. Only just in a formal, sentimental way. For old-time's sake. Nostalgia, for the superfluous being.

Al Lehman has made a monument to his old moral consultant. It's an ongoing monument. It's Al Lehman's acts. The lasting tribute.

XC. AL LEHMAN ARBITRATES A SUN-MOON DISPUTE. AS THE UMPIRE OR REFEREE IN THAT COLOSSAL TUSSLE, HE FAIRLY DOLES JUSTICE TO DAY'S GOLD ORB, TO NIGHT'S SILVER DEITY, IN DIVINE SKY'S DIVISION.

"Arbitrate a dispute between us," the sun and moon begged Al Lehman. "Sure, boys, stop bickering. Over what issue are you wrung in conflict?"

The sun started to speak, opening its golden mouth to that purpose. However, the smaller moon successfully cut in, with its darting silver tongue:

"Al Lehman, I have an inferiority complex in competition with the vastly superior sun over here. He's my sole adversary in the earth-portion of the sky, and so far outshines me that the difference is like that of night and day."

"Inevitably that must be so," Al Lehman adjudged, in gentle tones to that nocturnal orb. "Such a luminous body like the sun ought to illuminate your modesty, for it remotely forbids you no comparison at all. You derive secondary and reflected glory from that splendid orb. In yourself, pitiful moon, you're barely nothing, without that divine assistance."

These mocking tones by Al Lehman subdued and chastised the fiery little night-ball to a wan pallor, head hung in sorrowful humiliation.

Seizing this opportunity, the sun began to crow, in dulcet tones of divine-right supremacy, in the rolling brilliance of its grandeur: "Furthermore, moon, you're allowed to be seen only in gradual growth each month, and no sooner do you reach your fullness, but your new rotundity then begins to subside, falling back into emptiness by your pathetic phases of ebb. And should clouds hide you, base thing, at the time of your round glory, then you have to wait a month, poor thing, for that narrow opportunity once more."

The moon nodded. All this was perfectly true. The sun beamed, with its upper hand. It radiated, with contemptuous majesty.

Al Lehman saw fit to moderate. The sun's condescension so demeaned the poor moon, that the latter seemed faint and sick, about to die. Al Lehman stepped in, to abate the sun's cruelty and gently restore the sunken, limp confidence of the moon, who in this debate was being put in the dark shadow by his brilliant foe.

"Sun, don't rub it in," Al Lehman scolded. "Be a sport. Play fair. On a hot summer day, you drive millions of people to beaches in all states of undress. But the moon can drag the ocean tides, to push them out and pull them in, in currents of regularity. Give him credit, for that. Graciously congratulate him. You can afford to concede a point."

The sun did as Al Lehman bade. It shook the moon's flabby hand. A wave of restored confidence then overtook the moon. Resuming its pugnacious self, that mite of the night assumed the might of a knight in armor's glitter and gleam of high chivalry.

"Look, sun, don't be so dazzled by your fair self. In all your complacency, I was working to compensate for my inferiority to you. I cornered the market in the field of love and romance, and have a monopoly on it. Lovers swear by me, worship my shrine, in amorous nocturnal dalliance, in erotic moonshine, they moon over each other, these lovers, they're mine, I'm what's holy to them, in their chaste murmurings or hot delight. They pray to me, in the night. They hate when you end their lovely companionship in dark private beds together. Match *that*, you daily oaf!"

The sun slunk away, defeated. Al Lehman threw his arm around the moon, the referee awarding the victor his victory. The moon beamed. While the sun slept, he'd been busy in the night, becoming the God of love and romance. That hard work had paid off. He had rallied, to overtake the burly sun, as an essential human deity, love's primary "source," and the shadowy mover for dear romance, the shared illusion of the heart.

XCI. A STORY ABOUT THE WIND AND LEAVES THAT LEAVES THE LISTENER COLD, IF HE WASN'T THAT WAY BEFORE. THE PRE-ANTIDOTE IS TO READ THIS ANECDOTE INDOORS, IF POSSIBLE, EXCEPT IF THE WEATHER IS ALREADY WARM. THAT WAY, NO CHILL WILL GO DOWN YOUR SPINE, EXCEPT BY A CLOSE READING THAT SHUTS OUT OUTSIDE CONDITIONS IN SUBJECTING YOU TO AN AUTUMNAL ATMOSPHERE OF WIND AND LEAVES, STRIKING NUMB COLD INTO HUNGER'S WILD CORE.

"How can you explain a leaf? The leaf will stand for its own explanation, upon the tree of its context.

"A leaf symbolizes itself. It needs no further intermediator, for its existence to come across as poetry without benefit of metaphor."

That's what a poet said to Al Lehman. What reply could Al Lehman possibly make, to that? He tried: "I never wanted to 'explain' a leaf. As you say, it doesn't need one. Of course, it takes a lot of leaves to make one tree, above their trunk. That's a whole family, together. They cling together, even toward the end, in autumn. One autumn, they were getting frail and brown. A hard wind was blowing, it bore down, and used itself up with blowing, but then recouped somewhere, gathered itself together, and went howling through the trees, on a day that carouselled between sun and clouds, in brisk changes of the sky, high and stiff."

"Go on," begged the poet. "What's he leading to?" he asked himself, on the sly, as Al Lehman got ready to unleash the punch line from the base he'd been supplying.

"Well, the wind got exhausted, as well it might, having blown about all that day, and consumed more energy than it could renew. It was out of power, and needed nourishment. It gathered itself to rest, near the forementioned tree. 'I'm hungry,' it complained.

"The tree was sympathetic. 'I'll see what I can rustle up for you,' it offered; but couldn't rustle up any food at all, since the wind was too tired to blow any more."

"Did the wind die?"

"Yes, and so did that tree's leaves. Officially, winter had begun."

"Well, your story sent a chill down my spine."

"That's because you took it so personally, or too literally. Neither wind nor leaves were really people, you know."

"But they certainly *spoke* like people."

"That was for my *story's* sake. I endowed them with human speech, as an artificial convention in stylized fiction."

"If you hadn't, where would your story be?"

"Untold."

"And where is that?"

"Nowhere," said Al Lehman. He and the poet both were contemplating "nowhere." Neither, however, could get very far.

XCII. AL LEHMAN IS INTERVIEWED BY THE WORLD, UNIVERSE, OR SOCIETY, AND HIS REPLIES ARE TAKEN UP INTO THE COMMONWEALTH OF ALL HIS FELLOWS IN MANKIND'S MEMBERSHIP.

Asked for his comments on architecture, edifices, and air, including dirt, rocks, trees, and other elevations by nature from the bottom that stick out, protrude, and assert their shapes, Al Lehman went on record with this top-to-bottom, left-to-right, front-to-back, all-together reply:

"Actually, I don't know what I'd do without space; I'd really be at a loss."

"Yes, but what about *time*?"'insisted whoever interviewed him.

"Time? That's vital and essential. It's so necessary, I'd feel positively stifled, stuck, blocked, immobile, arrested, fixated, in fact paralyzed, without time's kind offices, which stretch things out and allow incomplete phases to get connected with penetration and thrust."

This seemed to satisfy the interviewer, but not for long. Recovering his oily air of ceremonious officialdom, he proceeded further to question Al Lehman on these topical matters:

"Yes, but. . ."

Al Lehman cut him short. "Why are you querying me? What's it to you, that my opinion is this about space, that about time? I'm not so famous as to justify your minute attentiveness to my casual notions."

"Yes, but. . ."

"Go on, explain yourself. Why have you hounded me, badgered me? Just whom do you represent? Are you exploitatively seeking to publicize my private inmost ideas and violate them?

You're a functionary. You're a worldly cheapener of what I hold dearly within me."

"Your inner life is not so sacred that it's to be held back from everybody else. The populace has a right to your privacy, which must be kept in open accessibility as eminent domain, public property, a collective belonging with connections to all minds, like books to be found on library shelves for anyone to come off the street and borrow."

"Am I a universal possession?" Al Lehman whined.

"Yes. I represent the outer world. Your own ideas are con-fiscated, co-opted, in deed and title; the rights to them go from you to all. The commonwealth claims those contributions of yours. Not merely space and time belong at large to everyone, but your own personal ideas about them, as well. You're not closed, but open, to your gregarious fellows, in the common chain or link, which extends you, in small membership, to the enormity of the flock, widespread and increasing. Don't deny your fellows. They won't allow you to. What's in you must come out. I'm prodding it, as an interviewer. I'm coaxing it. I wheedle information from you, extort or blandish, but extract. We're not plundering you. We regard you as a valuable resource, a mental outpost. Your findings. . ."

"My findings are by dint of my own work. They're the fruits of my labor. I reaped them by sowing."

"But this is a communal farm. Hand it all over, Al Lehman. Give. Partake. Contribute. For this booming largesse. This vast bounty, an organic unity, a body of collective humanity, com-prised of so many soul-cells, each a contributing member that feasts upon the gleanings of the rest. You have your place. It's linked, by local degrees, to the whole, by which it's nourished. Your place is yours, but ours. You're chartered a franchise. We own your work-and-play products. Time and space go on, with your ideas of them. Your universal productions are joined in by everyone. We all have a hand in you, in all your works. You enlarge our faculties that enlarge you. You're a man, within mankind. You add secretions, to the glandular Mind. It all leaks back to us; but we replenish you. We feed you space and time, for you to opine upon. What you say alters space and time. You hand back what you're given, worked upon."

"You enforce my joining. I'd rather keep it all to myself."

"That's selfish. We'll deprive you of space and time, if you don't cooperate."

"They're invaluable to me. Don't cut off those lifeline links to all of humanity."

"You've just spoken socially. Why, you're one of us!"

"But in spite of that, I'm an individual."

"That you are. The more individual you are, the more uniquely you contribute. We value your individuality. It's a rare contribution. It enriches us, you see. It's an uncommon contribution. It's highly regarded. We can well use it—and you. You're ours the more, for all uniquely that you give. Such rare endowments! We vastly benefit. Thank you."

XCIII. THE ATHEIST AND THE CHRISTIAN BE-LIEVER FIND GROUNDS FOR AGREEMENT: A WELL-REASONED WORLD.

"The unbelievable—literally unbelievable—stupidity and false-ness of the Christian myth, literally defies belief. . . unless you have faith. . . such faith as only stupidity and falseness could dredge up from their murky den of superstition."

This was addressed to Al Lehman by a confirmed atheist, in a tone of passionate cynicism, fervid disbelief. Al Lehman re-mained religious. What retort could he make, to such inspired negation?

The defender rose, chest forward, to declaim from might and power, using every inch of his height advantage and swelling shoulder spread, as if going for a basketball rebound with athletic dominance, instead of defending the faith by word of argumentative mouth to the full equality of their debate.

"I'm a Christian. Ours is no myth; still less a superstition; you accuse our credo of stupidity and falseness that you decry as unbelievable.

"But your position is false; your discrediting is stupid. *Your* negations are what *we* find to be unbelievable. Your postulates are irreconcilable with ours; there's no meeting ground, for dis-putation's fair waging on terms and planes for differences to branch from one field's agreed common frame of reference that sets spreading a scale rooted to comparison's single net, making possible the working out as applied to the measure of a struc-ture in key and code bound in honor to the same language, a system total for any appeal by the fair spirit of controversy."

Having said that, Al Lehman sat down like a man of reason rather than defender of the faith. The atheist sat down as well, close enough to Al Lehman for a ceremonious shaking of hands to dispel their vehement surge of opposition which had opened their fray in its defiant clash of fury.

Disbeliever and believer were reconciled. They resumed friendship. They shared the same earth, but knew well enough, now, not to let heaven come between them, to molest their friendly settling of a well-reasoned-out world.

XCIV. THE ATHEIST CONVERTS

"Were it not for religion, there'd be no atheism," a priest reminded Al Lehman. "As an atheist, acknowledge your debt and give religion credit."

"Yes, but why should I give *your* religion credit for *my* atheism? Atheism is true of any religion; it feeds on any religion. So stop converting me negatively."

"I'm not saying join my *particular* religion, or be obligated to it," was the priest's rejoinder. "I'm speaking for general religion itself."

"Are you entitled to? Haven't you sworn vows to your own special church, as its minister and interpreter?"

"But before that, I'm God's *overall* spokesman. There are ways and ways; faiths and creeds, church by church. Each church, each creed, each faith and way, all go back to one God; which we serve."

"Father, include me, in that wide unassorted flock, the unspecified worshippers."

"Glad to have you aboard, Al Lehman. On behalf of God Himself, let me welcome you."

"But Father, I already feel nostalgic for my atheistic days, which I renounced but one minute ago, as turncoat and renegade, deserter, abandoner, from my atheistic code. Such a traitor, I feel! I fear lightning would strike me down, in a divine wrath."

"God will protect you, Al Lehman. He controls the lightning. He'll order it to spare you."

"Thank God! Now, I'm safe!"

"Not just safe, Al."

"What else?"

"Saved."

"Saved? Good. I've been wisely deposited in God's roaring bank account?"

"It accounts for why you can bank on being saved."

"Will I draw interest?"

"Yes. God Himself takes a personal interest in you."

"That's flattering. I'll tell Him my life story."

"He already knows it."

"Such omniscience! Well, that's God, for you."

"For *you*, Al. He's for *you*."

"Me? But I'm so unimportant. A mere detail."

"God spares no details."

"Then what won't *I* be spared from?"

"From infinite mercy."

"Will I need it?"

"Sure. Watch how your life goes. See it unfold, bit by bit, in all that happens. You'll *need* all that mercy. And where will you get it? *God* is the supplier. You'll need *Him*."

"Who, though, is He?"

"Who *isn't* He?"

"That covers a lot of territory."

"It's God's province, to have the wide scope needed, to take intensive care of such extensiveness. You won't get *exclusive* care; you'll share it. But there's plenty there."

XCV. REMEMBER JENNIFER GROSSLOP? AH, MANY YEARS HAVE GONE BY, SINCE. LOVE IS STILL ETERNAL. BUT THE WOMEN CHANGE.

Jennifer Grosslop was gone, and Al Lehman was weeping.

She disappeared from sight forever from his life, kissing him weepingly goodbye and being seen, for the final time, going into the passengers' flight preparation tunnel, from there to board a plane that would wing her back to her native Britain.

Why hadn't it worked out, between them, here? It had begun so romantically, over there. He had been traveling there on a vacation, and met her through a friend's tea party introduction. But he only had a week left, before he had to return here to resume work.

Then, there followed a year of correspondence, of letters exchanged once a week, across the vast ocean, by air postage.

At one point, the letters were less frequent, and threatened to stop altogether. It seemed hopeless. They had only seen each other a few times, then all this correspondence, of pretty words. There wasn't enough substance, between them—nothing solidly established—to warrant her joining him here.

It was only a silly, romantic idea. Their lives were apart, in separate places. Why should she give up her roots, to be with him here? He had his professional career to carve out here. *She* had to come *here*, if they were to join lives at all.

The letter exchange waned. The matter was dropped.

A few months went by. Suddenly, a letter from her. Yes, she would reconsider what he had formerly urged her to do—but only if he *still* urged her to do it. Did he?

He wrote back: yes, he did. He adores her. Come live with him, here.

That did it. She wrote back agreeing. She would take her possessions with her, by boat. She booked an ocean liner. She said when the arrival date would be.

He prepared, to receive her. Would his apartment be to her liking? Would it be big enough, for her and him both?

She arrived. But she didn't like it here; meaning, she didn't really like *him* enough. They tried, for two months. Then she went back.

He still loved her, as she disappeared, forever, from his life into the flight preparation tunnel for air passengers at the lost airport.

With Jennifer Grosslop, he was a failure. However, next day, at the office, he met Marge, whom he married sometime later. A son Gregory kept them longer together than they would have been. Finally they parted, and divorced.

He had loved Jennifer Grosslop much more: they were only a short time together.

With Marge, it was *years* together. And ended badly.

New women, ahead. Put past failures behind. A middle-aged, divorced father. A new career: as a psychologist. Special post-graduate courses, just for that.

He counsels married couples whose marriages have hit on bad times. He knows about discord, disappointment, those delicate disillusionments.

Jennifer Grosslop, after long correspondence, had come by boat with possessions, ready for the new life, to uproot herself just for Al Lehman. She had her possessions sent back by boat, while she took the plane—she had to leave fast.

How sad. Al Lehman has gotten over her. The Marge marriage was disastrous, but he likes his son Gregory, whom he sees on the boy's holidays, taking him hunting, fishing, excursioning, money permitting.

In his new career, he's saved some marriages, but not others.

Why had Jennifer soured? Jennifer Grosslop.

What happened to her, back in Britain? There were no more letters, ever, from her. She never replied to his; which then stopped.

He'll live his life over. As before, all will be again. But better, the second time.

He'll erase the mistakes. He needs another chance.

No, that's just superstition. What happened, is done. New things are happening, later. No remedying, no patching up, the failures of before. He only has new starts. A new career. Some new women.

Love was Jennifer Grosslop. Love wasn't ever quite Marge. May his son Gregory know love with good endings; with nice outcome.

Death looms ahead. Not near, but far.

A lovely body fills his bed. The bed is sailing. Or, on wings, is a lofty plane.

His career is flourishing, as a psychologist. He's winning respect, in the trade.

He's older. But years lie ahead. And a lovely body, in his bed.

She's Louise, who loves him. She hears him mutter "Jennifer," in his sleep. She asks him who Jennifer was, when he wakes.

He tells her how long ago it was.

Louise leaves him. It was short-lived.

But Rosalie arrives. Divorced, with children. She's Al Lehman's latest love.

His last?

The years are stopping. But furiously fast.

XCVI. A WARNING, OR BROAD HINT, TO THE READER, THAT WHAT HE HAS LEFT TO READ HAS RAPIDLY DECLINED, WITH AN ABRUPT END GRADUALLY GROWING INTO SIGHT AS THE MATTER RUNS OUT TOWARD THE FINALITY OF THESE PAGES, THEIR DISAPPEARANCE INTO INCONCLUSIVENESS, WITH AL LEHMAN STILL UNKNOWN, AND LEFT RATHER GLARINGLY INCOMPLETE.

"I can write a book endlessly about you," said Al Lehman's potential biographer.

"Well, make a start," Al Lehman suggested.

The start has been made. The start's end, however, is now coming about.

XCVII.

(The final chapter, to be finally followed by the final title:)

A real writer could write about Al Lehman forever. That's because, as a subject, he's potentially inexhaustible. He doesn't have any finite definition. He doesn't have any definite character. He's unlimited by a specific personality.

Who, then, is he? Theoretically, a real writer could write volumes in answering that. Who, though, would venture to undertake so encompassing a theme, of such ambitious ambivalence?

What *has*, *actually*, been written of Al Lehman in this sketchy little book, barely scratches the surface of so broad and vast a subject as Al Lehman *could* lend himself to be. Such rudimentary, tenuous treatment he's received here, does his capabilities a severe injustice. He seeks, then, his ultimate biographer, through these bare beginnings, his tentative birth as an enduring character.

Should such author come along soon, Al Lehman is eagerly available, awaiting him. Longing to be *truly* known.

(The final title, finally, of the final chapter:)

THE FINAL CHAPTER ON AL LEHMAN—TILL THE AUTHOR COMES ALONG TO TRULY CONSUMATE HIM AS A CHARACTER, A FULLY ROUNDED CHARACTER EXHAUSTIVELY TREATED, DEFINED DEFINITIVELY, AND THOROUGHLY DELINEATED. TOWARD SUCH FULFILLMENT, HE'S HERE TRACED IN EMBRYONIC POSSIBILITY.

Marvin Cohen in the 1970s. Photo by Tom Gervasi

Marvin Cohen is an American essayist, novelist, playwright, poet, humorist, and surrealist. He is the author of nine published books and several plays. His short fiction and essays have appeared in more than 80 publications, including *The New York Times, The Village Voice, The Nation, Harper's Bazaar, Vogue, Fiction, The Hudson Review, Quarterly Review of Literature, Transatlantic Review,* and *New Directions* annuals. His 1980 play *The Don Juan and the Non-Don Juan* was first performed at the New York Shakespeare Festival as part of the Poets at the Public Series. Staged readings of the play have featured actors Richard Dreyfuss, Keith Carradine, Wallace Shawn, Jill Eikenberry, Larry Pine, and Mimi Kennedy. Born in Brooklyn in 1931, Cohen has described himself as one who has "risen from lower-class background to lower-class foreground." He studied art at Cooper Union but left college to focus on writing, supporting himself with a series of odd jobs including mink farmer and merchant seaman. He also taught creative writing at The New School, the City College of New York, C.W. Post of Long Island University, and Adelphi University. Cohen currently lives in New York City with his wife, a retired paperback editor.

www.ingramcontent.com/pod-product-compliance
Lightning Source LLC
Chambersburg PA
CBHW020400030726
47496CB00007B/2233